MOY McCRORY was born in Liverpool in 1953 to working-class parents of Irish origin. She grew up in Toxteth and was educated at the local parish church school and then at a convent school. She lived for a while in Northern Ireland and was a student in Liverpool and Belfast and later a post-graduate student in London where she now lives and works as a part-time teacher. She has a baby daughter, Katie-Ellen.

Her first short story to be published was 'The Water's Edge' in *Everyday Matters 1* (Sheba 1982), an anthology of short stories by women. Moy McCrory is now working on her second collection of stories based on women's fertility and is also busy researching a third book which is set in Ireland in the middle ages.

Photo: Jeremy Nicholl

THE WATER'S EDGE
AND OTHER STORIES

Moy McCrory

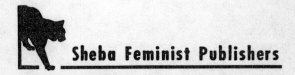
Sheba Feminist Publishers

First published in 1985 by Sheba Feminist Publishers
Second edition published in 1989 by Sheba Feminist Publishers
10A Bradbury Street, London N16 8JN

British Library Cataloguing in Publication Data
McCrory, Moy
The water's edge: and other stories.
I. Title
823′ .914[F]   PR6063.1655/

ISBN 0 907179 29 0

Photoset in Sabon 10/11½ by
PRG Graphics, Redhill, Surrey

Printed and bound by
Cox & Wyman, Reading, Berkshire

Contents

The Vision

Years ago while my mother was still a girl, one of the neighbours saw a vision. The Virgin Mary appeared in the back yard and when Mrs Daly went out to fetch the coal on Saturday morning she saw her as clearly as the nose on her face, standing out from the white washed wall by the coal shed. She was as large as life and, according to Mrs Daly's description, 'the very picture of herself all dressed in blue with a golden crown and smiling.'

She wore a blue mantle that the angels had lifted from a piece of the sky to gently wrap around her, carefully pleating into folds the hem of silver stars. Soft curling ringlets reached to her shoulders and she held a rosary of white pearl between her hands, which were joined in prayer. Her feet were small, dainty and quite bare as she stood on a tiny globe of the world, effortlessly crushing the head of the serpent underfoot; a gesture which recalled how she had vanquished evil.

Mrs Daly knelt down, overcome with emotion, not minding the filthy stone floor nor feeling the cold, although later that day she remarked that her rheumatism felt worse and that Our Lady must have been testing her.

At first the neighbours were sceptical but they gradually succumbed to curiosity. They knew well enough that the Virgin would not descend to earth without cause. She must have a special message for them.

'Did she say anything to you?'

'Did she ask you to pray for an intention?'

But the Virgin had been silent.

'She just stayed there looking around me yard. Maybe it made her homesick for the stable.'

'Didn't you ask her what she wanted?'

'Indeed I did not! I was struck dumb in the presence.' She placed her right hand over her heart and gazed upwards to wherever the Virgin had returned, hoping that she might receive a sign of approval.

That such a thing should happen in their street! The neighbours were all flushed with religious fervour and excitement. It was all that was talked about. Round every meal table all conversation was Mrs Daly's vision.

'Between you and me, I think she'd a wee drop taken,' said Mr Hanrahan to his wife as they sat slowly on at their Sunday breakfast.

'On a Saturday morning!' said Mrs Hanrahan in a tone which left him in no doubt what she thought of the idea.

'Well . . . ' he hesitated a little. 'Och, sure it could be lasting from the night before.' But his voice had no conviction.

'Well I can't see that.' His wife's voice was firm. 'She's not what I'd call a boozer.'

Mr Hanrahan avoided her eyes. He thought that she dwelt overlong on the word 'booze'. He hated that word with its mental picture of red swollen noses. Strawberry noses they were called. But he hadn't got that far himself. He put his hand up furtively and gave it a tweak, just to make sure that it had not grown into one since he had shaved.

'And she's not given to wild imagination!'

The hand swiftly withdrew. Sometimes, he thought, his wife was too perceptive. It was uncanny. He shifted uncomfortably in his chair and concentrated for a moment. Suddenly he lunged forward, spearing a piece of fried bread with his fork. He shook it several times demonstrating stability.

'Right enough,' he said as he stabbed the air with the morsel. 'She's a down-to-earth, honest, woman.' Three stabs of bread. Down-to-earth, stab, honest, stab, woman, stab and he quickly ate the evidence so that his opinion could not be sought again, or his version retracted.

'What about him? What does he make of it all?' She had to quiz him for the details which she had no access to herself. Who knew what a man may say in the bar? Her husband thought back to the night before. Mr Daly had been unusually quiet refusing to be drawn into conversation with any of them. He had hung back buying his own beer and standing alone.

'He's been awful close on the subject; he seems more embarrassed about it than anything.' Mr Hanrahan felt for the man — not everyone wanted to be married to a saint, or a lunatic, there wasn't often that much between one and the other.

'Oh God that's right,' said Mrs Hanrahan as an idea suddenly struck her. 'They could find her mad any day. He's hanging back in case his wife is three sheets. God knows what he'd do if she had to be sent away.'

'Aye, it'll be rough all right.'

They continued their breakfast, thoughtfully.

'Still,' he said brightening a little. 'Look at the way they laughed at Bernadette — said she was crackers and all the time she was a saint!'

Mrs Hanrahan looked at her husband, and gave him a smile of approval. 'You're a good man,' she nodded, and he, like a well-pleased child who knew he had said the right thing glowed with a dim pride and continued eating.

In the Clancy household the two youngest pestered their parents non-stop;

'Why can't we go round and look?'

'Because it's not a freak show!' yelled their father as he brought the flat of his hand down across one of them indiscriminately.

'I didn't say anything!' the recipient of the blow wailed.

'Don't then!' he warned.

'I'm not having you round there making fools of yourselves or of them, you never know . . . ' said their mother anxiously.

No one in the area was quick to denounce the vision, they were all too superstitious. But as the days passed and the Virgin was reported to have been seen on more occasions, this time by groups of people, more and more of them grew less embarrassed to be seen showing a keen interest. Eventually half the street was crowding into the yard in the hope of catching a glimpse.

They came round sheepishly at first.

'Just passing by and thought I'd drop in,' they said as their eyes stared past Mrs Daly searching hungrily.

'I'm going out there now,' she would say, taking the bait. 'Do you want to come with me?'

One by one the women would blush, stammer, and finally stand outside with her and the Virgin would appear. Every day there were more women who defied their husbands' orders and crept round while the men were at work. Some stood stiffly in the parlour while others dared to sit, balancing on the edge of the horsehair sofa with its graying antimacassars, their backs rigid. Even those who were close neighbours and old friends stared nervously at the china cabinet with its display of willow-pattern and the jug with 'A Present From Llangollen' trailed across it in slipware.

They sipped cups of tea, terrified to speak in case they were in the presence of the Holy. Only the bravest asked if they could go out into the yard. The rest waited for her to offer. Mrs Daly filled up their cups, extra charitably and offered them cushions to take outside.

'Our Lady doesn't want you all crippled with arthritis,' she said authoritatively as they hung back wondering if their penance would count so much if they did not suffer at least a little. One sentence from Mrs Daly and they complied. It was easy for her to instil awe into them. Even if she spoke figuratively she could not help but put words into the Lady's mouth.

'It's penance enough having swollen joints, Our Lady doesn't want you aggravating them.'

Chairs, kneelers and now even blankets were obediently carried outside. The women would follow meekly from the parlour that looked out onto the street, into the hall where the only light came from the thin-mouthed letter box that was permanently agape. Through it poured a shaft of sunlight turning the dust into spotlight flecks as it fell continuously on every surface. The women stumbled in the dark narrow passage, they tripped over the hatstand, knocking coats to the ground and, when they politely retrieved them, pricked their knees on the coconut matting.

Mrs Daly led them through the back room where everything smelled of bacon, cabbage and fried egg for all the past meals seemed to hang in the air. The women followed in procession, feeling silly and awkward. The cat no longer arched its back, although it sometimes attempted a soft growl. It was growing used to the file of people behind Mrs Daly. They had almost become an extension of its owner as it watched from the firegrate through slitted lids. In the kitchen the women were crushed together in the carbolic reek from the freshly scrubbed draining board. Sunlight caught the drips from the tap before they splashed into the gleaming porcelain sink.

There was something unnerving about a house which had been so obviously cleaned from top to bottom. Only new dishcloths hung behind the door and there was no washing on the line. It was as if the house was fast becoming unlived in, as the backyard grew into a shrine.

As its fame spread, more and more women came round during the day when their husbands were safely out the way at work. They went back to their old ways. Those who were bossy, bossed; those who were garrulous kept up a never-ending story. For, as time progressed and they had all had visions, they felt equal with Mrs Daly.

'Vision or not I can't have with all those wailing women out in the back! I'd like some peace when I come home from work, not that racket!' said Mr Daly as he crashed his lunch bag on the table and turned his back towards the window through which could be seen the kneeling forms of the pious ones who mounted daily vigil.

The kitchen was all bustle as cups of tea were steadily supplied to those who prayed throughout the day. The women had organised a rota, bringing five pounds of tea and a pile of shillings for the meter. He glanced angrily over his shoulder not wanting to give the impression of looking, but he saw the crude shrine that had been set up over the coalshed. His eyes took it all in; the white arum lilies scattered on the flagstones, the tin foil objects that had been twisted out of coat hangers, the crucifixes, the clean swept yard.

He looked on like a stranger while they brought rosarys and touched them against the wall. Holy pictures and missals that once they would have taken to the priest to bless, now they brought to the backyard. He felt uneasy. He did not dare go out the back way, which meant that he could not use the lavatory until the bulk of them had gone home to cook tea. Miracles and visions were all right but he didn't want them happening in his backyard. No disrespect, he added apologetically.

'Well I think it's wonderful that she chose our back yard to come into. Just think. She chose ours before anyone else's.' Mrs Daly blessed herself, feeling a warm glow. It was conceit to think that possibly she was better, more holy than the rest of her street, but . . . well . . . after all, it was *her* yard Our Lady had chosen. Yet lately Mrs Daly had begun to feel a bit peeved. Our Lady was not very selective about her audience. She seemed rather too free with her appearances to her liking. Still she had been the first to see her and that must have meant something.

The Virgin continued to appear, vague and shadowy and always silent, brooding on the fate of the world. But the moment the apparition slowly developed on the back wall was certainly miraculous. Even the most cynical could not have helped but been impressed by the rapt attention and singleness of purpose that was displayed as all the voices stopped mumbling for individual concerns and joined together in one solemn expression of faith. A gasp of wonderment went round and the bent heads were quickly raised from their beads. The gasp swelled and increased in volume, stretching itself out into a long wordless prayer. It was the sound of complete belief — and of hope.

They squinted up their eyes to make the indistinct image clear.

'Where is She?'

'There on the wall.'

'I can't see.'

And the experts who had been present at several sightings would point out how to follow the hem of the cloak and so trace the outline of the shadow.

'And there's her hands clasped in prayer. Follow the rosary beads up and you'll see them.'

'What, that triangle thing?'

'No, no. Just up a bit — can you see them now?'

Some of the neighbours never got beyond seeing just a dim shadow shape, while others claimed to have seen her face clearly and in such detail.

'Lovely long eyelashes she has,' someone muttered and others nodded sagely in agreement.

There was no gasp of wonderment or sound of hope in Mount Sinai presbytery. But there was the noise of Father Gormley as he tutted behind his newspaper. He rustled the *Catholic Pictorial* irritably as the housekeeper rushed into the study. Really she should knock! Lately she seemed to have lost all sense of propriety. He would have to have a word with her about it. And those silly tales she kept repeating! Already Mrs Clancy had gone up to young Father Morgan and was complaining loudly rather than say what she wanted to the more senior man directly. This was her way of attempting to draw him into the discussion.

'Well I think it's a disgrace,' she began, folding her arms across her chest and throwing her weight onto one leg. '*Those* women,' she said decidedly, having made up her mind that she was not one of them, '*those* women are making a mockery out of religion. As if the virgin would have nothing better to do than stand about in someone's filthy backyard!'

'But remember,' began the young man, 'that she had nowhere better to bear her son other than a lowly stable. Anyway it's not so much the place as the faith of the people that is important.'

'Och, not *those* people — not that mean, scruffy, fightin' lot. She would visit decent folk, honest people.'

'Well, well.' the young priest began in his reasonable voice, the one which he used for 'question time' after giving a talk in the parish school. 'To the humblest in turn Our Lord shares his bounty.'

Father Gormley put his paper down hotly. He felt uncomfortable.

'You're not telling me that you believe these stories?' he asked archly.

'No of course not,' the other said a trifle too quickly for his senior's liking. It was as if he had snapped. 'I was merely disputing a point — that the good Lord belongs to the lowest as well as to the highest. We are all equals in the eyes of God.'

He stroked his gingery hair which was the sign that he was getting into his stride. Father Gaughan blanched. 'It makes one think,' he continued. 'There is, after all, no reason why such things cannot happen unless you belong to that school of thought which claims that the entire bible is allegorical. Certainly the saints' fables of the middle ages are, with one mind, put down as folklore. But the loaves and fishes, the water into wine, the Virgin birth . . . are we to discount these?'

The old priest stared hard at the young man. What were they learning in the seminarys these days? To him it was clearcut. An hysterical woman was creating a potentially embarrassing situation for him.

'I'll put a stop to this folly!' he muttered as he rose stiffly from his chair. 'I'm going down there now to see what all this fuss is about.'

Later that day Father Gormley arrived in the district armed with holy water and his missal. He hated house calls there in particular. It was not only his priesthood that made him different from those people, but his whole manner and bearing. His speech was not the same, and he felt awkward. Not that these people didn't welcome him, not at all. It was the excess of the welcome which embarrassed him more than anything. The best plates, the best cups, the carefully hidden piles of newspapers and rubbish thrown under the settee when they saw him approach. When he had started in that Parish he used to wonder at the strange method of furnishing that was so popular. The chairs with high cushions that he sat on, his feet not quite reaching the ground. Then he realised that he sat on top of piles of clothes, nappies, papers all speedily hidden under seats. He could well imagine how a cry went up at the back of the houses. Over walls they passed the word. Children were sent running to warn relatives.

'Jasus! Get that bloody dog out the kitchen and look you, pull yer braces up.'

'You'd better be gettin' them false teeth in yer head, the priest's on his way over.'

Something in him yearned to not always play the role of the formal visitor, but something equally repelled him from a greater intimacy.

He had difficulty finding the street. There were so many, in such a small space and they all looked the same. He turned a corner and was utterly lost. He turned back past the dairy into a narrow side street and asked a group of children where the street he searched for was. The kids were excited by the prospect of leading the priest to the shrine and walked with him feeling important. All the local children knew about the shrine. Some had started selling bits of the brick wall to hapless pilgrims, despite Mr Daly chasing them whenever he heard 'chip-chip' from the entry.

'The bloody house will fall down next!' he cursed, storming into the kitchen. Mrs Daly blushed. Fancy using language like that when Our Lady might be present!

'Sod Our Lady!' he blasphemed, stamping his way upstairs.

His wife clutched her heart as if stricken.

'Forgive him Holy Mother. He's under a lot of stress, he doesn't know what he's saying.'

Alone in the bedroom he waited patiently for the thunderbolt to strike, unaware that his wife had interceded for him.

But the parish priest had been just as bad.

'No, no, NO!' he said, 'the Virgin would not just appear, not just like that,' snapping his fingers like a conjuror. 'Not in that way,' and he picked his way distainfully through the yard which, although it had been steadily disinfected, still smelt of cat.

'Jealous!' Mrs Daly said after he had gone. 'That's what he is — because the Blessed Virgin chose to appear in my yard and not in 'is rotten church.'

'That's right luv,' one of the women said. 'They want to keep everything to themselves those 'oly ones. Don't want anyone to share the miracles.'

The neighbours were all united.

'It's a trick of light,' the priest had tried to tell them. 'Just a trick played by light and shadows,' and he had urged them all to return to their homes.

'Just because he couldn't see Her he reckons no one should!'

So they remained, more fervent than ever. 'She's only appearing to those she wants. She won't appear for sinners.'

Everyone began to have clear sightings. Even those who for long had insisted that they could not make much out suddenly began to see the image clearly. Plain, solid, impossible to be mistaken.

'Like a photograph,' they said.

Attendance at Father Gormley's weekly confession dropped dramatically. They knew that Our Lady had come down to them, the common ordinary folk. They were the real saints, they who had all the struggle bringing up kids and trying to make ends meet. They couldn't pass a plate round once a week and expect it to be filled. No, they were the real saints. It was all right for the clerics to come round in their black robes and look down on them, tut-tutting because someone was pregnant again. And the nuns were worse. Mrs Daly despised them. She thought that they were bitter, lonely and twisted. They had made her daughter miserable at school by poking fun at her asking the 'girl whose mother sees visions' to read, instead of using her name. She knew that all the other girls at school must have stared at her daughter, lapping it up.

The street was closing its ranks, fearful of outsiders who might come to mock. They turned strangers away from the back door unless someone could vouch for them. 'She's me mam's second cousin, she's got a special intention to ask' might gain an audience.

One weary pilgrim who had travelled all the way from Birkenhead on the bus was turned away, and many had to content themselves with buying souvenirs from the kids that hung about the back entry, or in touching the outside of the wall. Some lay stretched out in the entry prostrating themselves with all the rubbish.

'They don't care what germs they pick up. They go home all covered in muck,' the neighbours said in surprise, shaken by such display.

The mania lasted for almost a fortnight. Later, when the event was wound up completely, not mentioned anymore, people wondered why it had dragged on for so long before the discovery was made. But for years after, the newsagent could not be persuaded to re-order after he changed his stock. He was the Catholic newsagent supplying all the catholic papers, pamplets, books and artifacts that were sold at the back of the church on Sundays. In his window he displayed a range of statues, there was Saint Theresa beautified, Blessed Martin De Porres, the boy Jesus, but he would not be persuaded to re-order the glass statuettes with safety night lights despite the sales rep's efforts.

'They're great little sellers these. They're going mad for them in Saint Bernard's, them and the velveteen mass cards. Go on! You won't regret starting with them again.'

But the man always refused. The commotion caused by one such statute was still too sharp in his memory. They had been good sellers, especially the Madonna with crown standing on the globe of the world. These statues had an unusual feature. If the night light was lit it shone through the figure and illuminated it. Some clever souls had discovered that by placing a convex mirror behind, or a bowl of water, which was a trick the lace-weavers of old used, the statue would be shown in an enlarged reflection on the opposite wall.

Mrs Daly felt so foolish when the storm broke, that something so simple could have been the cause of such profound experience. Why had she not turned around on that fateful Saturday and looked straight over to the house behind? She would have seen the statue surely? But she had been too respectful to turn her back on the vision. She felt angry with herself. Gullible fool!

All the pilgrims disappeared as quickly as they had arrived, leaving not a rosary bead behind. They went back to their houses feeling contrite and ashamed, leaving Mrs Daly to survey the wasteland of her yard. Where once there had been excitement there was now only a backyard, cold and uninviting.

'Didn't I say from the start that it was nothing?' her husband said as she dragged her feet across the kitchen.

'God curse you, you old heathen!' she flashed angrily. 'Just you try and come the know-all with me. You didn't want it happening in your yard that's all you said!' and she stormed past him.

People were quick to claim that they had never really been taken in by the affair. Everyone sought a way to keep face.

'Well you know, I never really saw a thing on that wall they were all staring at.'

'No, no, I never could. Funny that.'

'There were shadows though and I suppose with all those people around, well, we never got to the front of the crowd did we?

'No. I can't see anything over a distance. Me eyes, you know.'

'And everyone shouting and carrying on like that out in the kitchen . . . '

'Not very religious I thought . . . '

But after a while people no longer bothered to justify themselves. Instead there grew up an unspoken agreement that the incident should no longer be talked about, that it should be allowed to die out as naturally as possible. On the surface there was a return to normality and the infallibility of the church. Its correctness was a finger pointing towards their unorthodoxy. Not quite heretics these simple folk, but in their delusion they had set up their golden calf.

To Father Gormley it all smacked of insubordination. They needed the rigid discipline of the church to keep control, he would permit no liberties. But his conscience was sorely troubled. Had he unwittingly caused such an absurdity by misteaching? Had he been too trustful in their understanding as they chanted Latin prayers, a gabble of voices on Sunday? Was it his fault that his parish had been singled out for such a shameful blunder?

Behind closed doors there was anger. Every home felt cheated. Their faith had failed them. They had been within reach of a miracle, right out of church. It had waited for them on street corners, hovered on their doorsteps quitting the holy places for the backyards and mean pushed-together houses. But they had been wrong in their apocryphal vision and the church had been shown once again, unimpeachable, correct. Miracles were the prerogative of those who had made a career from them.

As confession began to pick up slowly again even Father Gormley noticed a change of their manner.

'There's a defiance in their voices,' Father Morgan said excitedly after morning confessions.

There was something almost irreligious about them.

'They need to learn the lesson of humility still,' Father Gormley said. And he cast his cold eye over those who had nearly been saints.

'The Vision' appeared in *Escape Magazine* no. 7 as an illustrated story entitled 'The Toxteth Madonna'.

Last Judgement

'So we always love our Mummies just a little bit more than our Daddies because it is our Mummies we see first when we are born as tiny babies,' Miss Thomas said.

Miss Thomas was the first year infant teacher at Our Lady of Mount Sinai Parish Church School, where I was sent at the age of four and was to remain until I was eleven. She taught the new entrants and felt that she had the hardest job because she had to win us for the school, coaxing us away from home in those first tearful days. But she believed that she was closer to us than any subsequent teachers having won the initial battle for our hearts.

She believed that to 'catch them young' was the only right way to go about educating us. For if she set us on the right path in those early years she knew that we would remain God-fearing and pious for ever. She saw her duty clearly. It was spiritual. If she looked after our souls everything else would take care of itself. Day by day she delighted in her task, pounding us into shape. It all seemed so simple, so straightforward. Everything had an explanation and she would supply it. Everything started with God.

Miss Thomas was our mentor and our light, she was the fund of knowledge to which we all returned, time after time.

'Miss Thomas will know.'

'Ask Miss Thomas.'

And while the rest of the staff were known by nicknames, she remained, always Miss Thomas.

It could not have been easy being a teacher in that school. There were constant inspections made by the church and governors, who kept a close watch on precisely what was being taught and how. The correct line on faith had to be adhered to. So we spent a lot of time praying and reciting hymns and learning our catechisms for surprise tests that these visiting powers were fond of springing on us. Any teacher could be removed from their post if the visiting panel was displeased with his or her performance.

'This class is very weak on the Holy Trinity. It ought to be learnt.'

The poor teacher in charge of that class would spend the next fortnight drilling her charges in the Three in One and the constant mysteries. Small wonder that the public examinations were, without fail, disappointing. We put so much energy into demonstrating our moral superiority we had little time left for mathematics.

I think it rather suited Miss Thomas because, deep down she had little talent for teaching and even less factual information to divulge. I suspect that she knew not even the rudiments of grammar, nor how to teach us even to play in a constructive manner.

We sat in twos on desks with fixed seats that we could not move, for they were bolted into the side of the table legs. This meant that I could never sit closely enough to the desk to feel comfortable. On the wall were number charts or counting charts which were a series of spots in uniform order. Miss Thomas would point with a stick and we would count up the spots aloud.

Apart from being frequently bored by her lessons, the other most common reaction to her was the feeling of guilt. She was fond of pronouncing some truth and following it up with an impossible demand. Like on the occasion that she told us that no matter what we felt for our parents we had to love God more. It was an unreasonable demand to make of a class of four year olds. Not that it was difficult to imagine God, the classroom was full of pictures of him. He was a white man that wore a flowing skirt and had a beard and long wavy hair. Although I knew of no one else who dressed like that, he did not strike me as peculiar. Perhaps because he was all-seeing and all-powerful he had been awarded carte blanche for his personal habits.

'You must love God even more than your Daddies, even more than your Mummies.'

'Whenever Miss Thomas made a statement she had the habit of going round the room to solicit our individual agreement, as if canvassing for votes.

'Do you, Dominic?'

'Do you, Bridget?'

She addressed each child in turn, waiting for the nod of the head and the words 'Yes, Miss Thomas' before continuing her journey.

At the age of four I must have had a conscience, for that day stands out in my memory. I was having trouble. Doubts were nagging me. How could I possibly love someone more than my aunt or my parents on whom I depended for just about everything? Would God help me to tie my shoelaces or put elastoplast on my knee?

'God is a spirit. He is everywhere. He is here now, only we cannot see him,' Miss Thomas said.

I tried to imagine it. Would it be like living with the invisible man if he should suddenly turn up at home? Would I have to help him in the morning by holding his bandages as he wound them tightly around himself? I fretted. Life would have been easier if I could have answered 'yes' and let the inquisitor pass on, but Miss Thomas had taught us too well that each day might be the one on which God was going to test us. I prayed that the school would spontaneously burst into flames and I would be saved, but unfortunately I was to be tested.

Her voice was harsh, staccato.

'What do you mean, you're not sure? Either you do love God, or you don't.'

There was a cavernous silence. I was speechless with terror. Nothing I could say would redeem me, I was already sunk without hope.

'You are telling us that you do not love God.' Miss Thomas's voice echoed in the silent classroom. I remember well the blanched faces of the other children, shaken in the presence of a heathen.

'Children, we have someone in our midst who does not feel the same way as the rest of us do about God. Someone who refuses to put God first and commits the same sin as Lucifer. Someone who refuses to acknowledge His power, His greatness. Why, He could destroy this person with one tiny movement from His little finger! But does He? No! Even while she defies Him, His love is all forgiving!'

Her eyes became moist as she got into her stride.

'In the struggling army of little saints,' she continued having cast her eyes approvingly around the room at the upturned faces, 'in our little army, someone feels that they can do without the love of God. They have decided that they do not need it!'

She pointed a finger at me.

'*She* would rather be damned to live and rot in Hell for ever and ever, being eaten alive by snakes and vipers, with fire burning her feet to a revolting molten mass . . . isn't that so?' She smiled sweetly as she asked me the question.

Sweat glistened on my forehead. I could feel the heat from the fire. My face glowed in its burning orange light. I thought carefully. How could I honestly say that I loved God more than family? It was a different feeling.

'Well, do you love Him more than your parents?'

Eternal horrors waited for me. I would have to love God because he was on the side that was winning. But it was not honest.

Thirty-four small faces turned on me imploringly, thirty-four pairs of eyes begged me to stay on the straight and narrow.

I wondered how I would ever get through the day without retracting. The next few hours loomed bleakly ahead. I saw myself being made to come forward in front of the entire school. I saw the placard being hung around my neck announcing my transgression. On Sunday I would be made to stand apart from the faithful. The priest would sprinkle me with holy water, being careful not to come too close. The water would hiss and steam as it splashed on the fiery turmoil that was my soul. No one would be allowed to play with me. Mothers would carry their sleeping babies indoors from out of their prams whenever they saw me approach. Doors would slam in my face. Our home would be marked, the home of an eternal damnation. My mother would be shunned at the green-grocers, my father at his workplace. How could I be so selfish? If God was prepared to go to such extremes to win I would have to give in.

As I walked home that afternoon I did not bless myself as I passed the church, which was our custom. I was daring God to do something, to call be back, make me walk home the rest of the way on my knees. I didn't care. I felt reckless. I felt he owed me something after the tight corner he had let me get into that afternoon. He had been watching while I squirmed and tried to talk my way out of it and prayed for the miracle that he never sent. He knew as well as I did that I had lied in the end. I was forced to, just to end the lesson. I may have fooled Miss Thomas but there was no kidding him. If he knew all along that I was just fobbing her off then why had he not stepped in to help me? He didn't make these silly demands on me, he already knew the answers and tolerated us because we were his children, and we all knew that God loved children best.

With Miss Thomas I asked only for a quiet life. So, eventually, I had to agree with her. A lie. I confess. But God knew all along and could have prevented my sin. Why hadn't he?

I was angry with him as I stalked defiantly past the church door. Still waiting for a sign, I turned back to cross the path again, this time glaring at the brickwork as I did so. But still nothing. People were walking past me, crossing themselves as they went. Over the road people still blessed themselves as they came out of the newsagents. I felt emboldened by all these signs, which made my failure to perform it seem all the more daring.

'I love my mother, my father, my aunt, and my cat much more than you,' I thought clearly. And I repeated it slowly twice to myself, so that he might have no difficulty picking up the message.

A Quick Sale

It was only after my father was dead that we discovered that the house in which we lived had a cellar. That extra space had been my father's jealously guarded secret. He got down into it by a trap door that opened up in the floor and was always covered over by lino. Not that he needed to cover it over for it was in the shop, an unused part of the house that had become my father's den and into which none of us had the right to go.

Some of the older neighbours remembered that the shop had once been a butcher's, but that was a long time before my mother and father moved in and it stood empty for years.

My mother never wanted to live there. She did not like the house right from the start. The only thing that made her feel optimistic was the thought of opening up the shop. My father talked about it creating a job at home for her and she thought fondly of a little drapers selling wool and sewing threads, but she never liked the house. It was ungainly, built on a corner which meant that it was in two streets and did not really belong in either.

It was separated from the other houses by a narrow entry on one side and a junior school on the other. It looked bigger than the rest, but this was chiefly because the length of the house faced onto the street. The others were turned the other way and presented only a narrow exterior while their living areas went back from the street.

Downstairs it was very cramped. There was a tiny front room and an even smaller parlour, and no kitchen, only a small pantry with a stone sink and one tap and enough space to fit a small cooker. The empty shop took up all the space. But he talked so much of how the house could be improved by 'modernisation', of walls being knocked through and an extension for the kitchen until she was persuaded that it was a good idea and all the savings that he had brought with him from Ireland, plus whatever she could contribute, went into buying the house.

For the first two years the house was uninhabitable and my mother stayed down the high street where her sister and brother and brother's wife lived. That was a tiny place, five adults were trying to fit into two bedrooms when my mother produced yet another person, her baby son. I suppose she must have anticipated the day when she would at last move into her own home and be the woman of it, but there was so much work that needed to be done first. Seamus, her brother, used to go up in thé evenings and the two men would work on it. But more often than not he came back shaking his head saying that it was too much for anyone to do on their own.

My father was taking all the joists out and trying to re-align new ones. Skilled jobs about which he knew nothing. He reckoned that he had the builders' skills inherited from the tradition of building farms overnight, raising outhouses and daubing walls with mud. But this was the middle of the city and things weren't like that. Then he discovered that the joists had dry rot and the framework of the house was collapsing, but he carried on. He refused to admit that he had made a mistake and would not agree with Seamus, who said that he would be better to cut his losses. Bill had signed all the contracts without getting advice, and he was tied, mortgaged. He must have thought that it reflected badly on his manhood, because he would not discuss it and he made Seamus promise not to tell Nell.

After two years of waiting she wanted to go and live there. 'It can't be that bad,' she insisted. But the first time she went up to look around properly she found all the upstairs doors locked.

'They're not ready yet,' he said. 'The floorboards aren't laid.'

'But we'll need a bedroom for Brendan,' she said.

'Oh Christ, give me time,' he said. 'Just give me time.'

When I was only a small child my father was a shadowy figure that I seldom saw. He rose and left early in the morning to return only after I was asleep. When he was at home he would don his white dustcoat and go into one of the many locked rooms in the house where he would spend whole days. I was only ever aware that it was the weekend because his coat and boots would be in the hall.

He collected things and remodelled old parts of machinery trying to get broken things to work again. He prided himself that he was an inventor and presented my mother with home-made labour-saving devices which never lived up to his claims about their performance.

In time the things that he collected for his hobby took over the house. Two bedrooms upstairs had been filled before my brother or myself were born, the shop was packed out and the parlour was starting to fill up. The floorboards and the joists had all been replaced, but still these rooms remained locked. At first he had brought wood home to fix the floor, but long after that had been finished there were still planks of wood lying about everywhere. And junk, because that's all it was really. Nell wondered if she imagined it or was it becoming so that wherever she turned there was more stuff piling up. He filled the house up until none of the rooms were empty. They were full with bits of electrical machinery that he was going to fix up; parts of cars that he could never drive; cogs, wheels, valves; old television sets; refrigerators — anything that he might be able to restore to life.

Nell said that it was a mania with him, some men gambled or drank, her husband did neither but he collected things. He hoarded. She said that the house was like living in Paddy's market*. Occasionally she would take down the key from where he hung it over the mantelpiece and trembling as if to find Bluebeard's most recent wife, would creep along the passageway to sneak a look at his acquisitions.

Nell hated going into those rooms. They all had the same terrible unlived-in atmosphere, and everything was filthy, covered in oil and dust. There was so much clutter and the damp smell got into her hair and clothes and she felt that she could smell it everywhere, as if the rooms followed her round for the rest of the day. If she shut her eyes she saw the piles of junk that were upstairs over her head. One day those ceilings would come crashing down under all the weight, for the stuff was piled up from floor to ceiling. Old furniture that he was supposed to be mending, chairs with legs missing, old cupboards that became full up with more junk before the original defect was seen to, broken crockery, saucepans without handles, broken binoculars, lenses from a lighthouse, barometers, an assortment of wire and string that hung from rusty nails in the walls.

*Great Homer Street market in Liverpool.

Some old 78 records, that he had bought at an auction, lay in one room in heavy stacks that stood waist high. They were useless, unplayable, with dirt engraved in the grooves. He was fixing up an old gramophone with a handle that turned. There were telescopes, a microscope without the focusing knob, a wooden box full of glass plate negatives that he'd picked up somewhere, a broken tripod, an old camera with a moth-eaten black curtain, an enlarger that did not work but he was mending, boxes of broken tools, an assortment of rusted sculptor's blades, a selection of wooden and leather-bound boxes whose hides had split, and lots of other things that were just unrecognisable. It was impossible to walk around in the rooms because of the amount of paraphenalia, but she walked through the stacks following the narrow path that he had left between the columns.

I remember being dwarfed by great pieces of machinery, all of it mysterious for I never knew which machines had yielded which parts, nor could I imagine their eventual purpose when my father had finished with them. They were all harbingers of dust and dirt. I remember only too well the peculiar smell in those unlived-in rooms and the thin film of dust that fell softly onto everything and coated all the surfaces with a grey tracery. If I spent just a few minutes in any of those rooms my hands would always be filthy and the rims of my nails blackened after I came out, and I had breathed in a stale airlessness of rust and waste and decay. The rooms were always bitterly cold and the only light in each came from a bare, weak bulb. More often they were in darkness except for the solitary beam from an overhead lamp where my father sat tinkering, happy playing with his machines or sorting through bottles of chemicals. But even during the day, when my mother went timidly exploring, there was hardly any light because the windows were filthy. She could not get near to them and so they never got cleaned on the insides. Little daylight could ever filter in through the layers of grime. The light bulbs gave everything a yellowish tone. The walls, which had been stripped of wallpaper and coated in lining paper years ago when he had first started work on the house, were dirty and sickly looking under the bulbs.

She never knew how he could bear to think about the things that were behind those locked doors. They gave her the horrors, and stopped her sleeping at night. But it didn't affect him, and he didn't see that this hobby was making her ill. When she had first known him he had had a workshop, but more the way men had garden sheds. This wasn't like that anymore.

She felt that she could not confide in anyone outside her family because they would all talk about her behind her back and feel sorry for her. She couldn't bear that.

'There goes Mrs Mac. Do you know that they sleep in one room because he's got the others all full up with junk?'

'Really!'

'God it's unhealthy that!'

'Those poor kids haven't got anywhere to go or run about in.'

Oh no! She couldn't bear that. Have them looking at her pityingly every time she went to the shops. So it became her guarded secret. She could never get too friendly with anyone because she couldn't ask them inside. And people must have wondered, because it was a bigger house than the others.

Even when she tried to clean up the parlour by heaving boxes and stacking them into the corner to get at the lino with a wet mop and dust around tins and over planks of wood she knew that her efforts made little difference, and they made no impression on him. He was impervious to her misery.

'I can't bring anyone home,' she sobbed. 'Not without a front parlour to take them to.'

He would look at her dumbly. 'Well don't bring anyone home then. I can't see that that's a problem.'

For him it wasn't. He didn't like people. He never socialised with the men from the factory and couldn't bear to have visitors. 'Why do they always turn up while I'm eating? I can never get a meal in peace,' he sulked.

Except for Nell's family, very few people did call round and he wasn't happy with that particularly.

'There isn't one of your mother's family that's worth bothering with,' he once said to me. 'The only one I had any time for was Seamus, God rest him.' He did not mind people quite so much once they were dead.

'The miserable bastard! He doesn't give a damn that the kids can never bring their friends home because there's nowhere for them to go. I can't let them go to any birthday parties because we'd be expected to invite the others back, and they can't have parties here. Because he's anti-social we're all being made that way.'

He always told us that he was an orphan and had no family. My mother used to say that she would not have been surprised if he'd made it up, just to spare him from having to spend any time with them.

'Those poor kids with him for a father,' Aunt Margaret always said. She never understood why her sister had married the man, and he did not like Margaret so there was no love lost between them. They treated each other to an icy politeness if they ever spoke, but they spent most of their time avoiding each other. Margaret used to visit Nell when he was out at work.

Nell was secretly relieved that he worked such long shifts. For although it was ageing him too quickly it gave her liberty during the day. Liberty to stand in the parlour surrounded by rusted junk and worthless rubbish and cry. Liberty to shout and scream and throw things at the walls. She would nag and nag at him and he, in turn, would shout and yell and threaten to sort out the stuff and get the parlour decorated and the house 'modernised'. But nothing happened and he kept bringing home his bargains. It wasn't fair, Nell could not stop him. It was his money, he went out to work and earned it and he could spend if as he liked.

He handed over the housekeeping promptly every Thursday night, always the same amount for years. She never knew if he'd had a rise and although he did a lot of overtime she never got to see any of it. She always had to ask him for money and he'd make a big fuss, and she had to eke out the housekeeping. She hadn't had anything new for ages and daren't ask for money to go to the hairdressers as her hair went progressively grey with worry. She felt a mess. She began to hate him and everytime he brought something else in and hoarded it in the parlour it was as if he had slapped her face. Once she picked up the shovel and waved it threateningly at his head. But the terrified look on my face must have stopped her.

Margaret came into the house one day to find Nell upstairs stretched full length on the bed sobbing as though her heart was breaking.

'Don't let him get you down, love,' she said.

'But I can't go on like this,' my mother cried, 'every room is full of rubbish.'

At this stage we were all sleeping in the same room, the two other bedrooms being full of machinery, and we had one room downstairs. Two rooms to live in out of the entire house. The rest of the rooms were out of bounds to us children, and locked against my mother. She took down the key and went around flinging the doors open, feeling reckless, so that Margaret could see in.

'Look at this,' she said with an elegant sweep of her hand. I remember feeling that mother was betraying a confidence.

'And don't you go saying anything to your father,' Margaret told me wagging her finger in my face. 'Do you hear me?'

'What am I going to do when the kids get bigger?' my mother was asking. 'They can't stay in the same room with us. I'm terrified in case anyone finds out. I could never bring anyone in here. If the priest calls, sometimes I go down on me hands and knees out in the pantry so that he won't see me through the window. I can't be bringing him in with the junk all over the house and the mess the place gets into.

'I clean it, I'm always cleaning and putting things away, but it's the only room in the house that we live in and we do everything here. The kitchen is so small that I make all the food through here, we eat here, I do me ironing here, there's always clothes on the maiden drying. I do all me mending and sewing here so the sewing machine is out on the sideboard. I try to keep all me bits and pieces tidy, all me boxes of cotton and pins and the wool bag is there for me knitting.

'And he comes in and reads the paper and puts the telly on, and the kids play there and all their toys are out over the floor. And last night he brought home the inside of a washing machine and just left it sitting by the armchair and we all had to step around it. And I asked him what the hell did he think he was playing at and he said it was only there temporarily, because there was no room for it anywhere else. I ask you, three rooms full of junk and now he's starting to fill up down here!'

She was shaking and crying. 'I can't go on like this, the miserable bastard! Oh God forgive me!'

'There, there,' said Margaret, putting an arm around her.

'Temporary!' Nell spluttered. 'Temporary! I've heard that one so many times before. Oh, Margaret if he carries on like this there won't be any room left for us to live in. He's sqeezing us into a corner, all of us. How can the kids grow up here? There's no room for any of us to stretch. They don't notice yet, they're still little.'

But it was already affecting us. Before I started school I remember being drilled by my mother.

'If anybody asks you a question, say that you don't know. If they ask you about this house, say that you can't remember.'

She was terrified that I should, in my naivety, tell the teachers the awful secrets of the house. And the teachers in turn must have wondered why I was so silent. I sat terrified of speaking in case I blurted out the awful facts.

'Take your drawings home,' they told us, 'and you can put them up on your bedroom wall.'

We were all in one room with the beds jammed end-to-end. There was no wall that wasn't shrouded by high wardrobes or one thing or another. I left my drawing where it was.

'She's not interested in her schoolwork,' the teachers said. 'She takes no pride in the results.'

'We'll sort something out, we must,' Margaret said thoughtfully.

It must have been shortly after this that she galvanised my mother into action. She still had her dream of opening a drapers, so Margaret found out the addresses of some and took my mother along. I remember how they came back, excited, with paper bags full of button-cards and samples of wool and thread and yards of elastic in different widths. Fondly they sorted through them on the kitchen table, piling them up and mother smiled at me and talked about 'our shop' and the things we would have in it. I played with the cards, counting the white shirt buttons that were stitched on in neat rows of threes. They fingered the fabric critically, opening out the swatchbooks to examine the quality under the light.

'This is a good winter weight,' my aunt said and mother made a note in a small red notebook that she had bought from Woolworths that day.

They glowed with satisfaction at their achievement, still believing that the shop would be a reality.

'What about the shop?' she reminded him that night and he began to move all his stuff over to one side and build a rickety wooden counter.

It was a start. But when he understood what mother wanted, which was to have Margaret helping out, because she was never able to keep a job on account of the headaches and this way she would be able to work whenever she was able, and when he understood the nature of the shop, he sulked.

He didn't speak for days and was bad tempered with us. He told her that he wanted to open a second-hand shop, and she grimaced and said that he really meant a junk shop. A scruffy, dirty, pokey little shop where old men with crooked backs liked to spend the afternoons fidgeting among the ruins. It would be like having a rag-and-bone yard.

'What about the drapers?' she asked him.

'Oh stuff your bloody drapers and your bloody sister!' That was what had annoyed him the most. 'She's behind this, she thinks she'll be the manageress. Well I'm not ever paying that idle woman wages. She can't keep a normal job. She's no bloody use.'

'What in God's name can you mean by that? She's up here more days than enough, helping me with the kids.'

'Oh yes?' he said cynically. 'What does that entail? She comes up here and drinks tea, that's all she does and plays daft bloody games with them. She's lonely, that's why she's here. Tell her to stay in her own bloody house. We don't need her here.'

The shop never opened. Each one blamed the other for this. He said that she had stopped him. Once in a while she would get out the button-cards that were faded and yellow and tied up into neat bundles. She would sit looking at them, knowing that if he had really wanted a junk shop he would have gone and done it. He didn't need her permission. He hadn't when he had bought the house.

Sometimes she would yell at him. They were building modern council houses by the Dingle shore, with gardens. She wanted to put their name down, but every time she mentioned it he went crazy and shouted her down.

'And you couldn't knock a nail in without permission,' he'd shout.

'Aye and you couldn't fill it up with all that bloody rubbish.'

So the shop remained unopened, the doors remained locked to the bedrooms and Nell continued to struggle to keep what little space was allowed to us tidy.

We liked my father. He was a comic character although he never meant to be, but his antics were a great source of amusement. He was of a scientific turn of mind and he fancied himself as an inventor. He re-made and re-modelled perfectly adequate designs for household implements which he then got my long-suffering mother to try out. Experiments. He dabbled with chemicals, ever hoping to discover some new scientific principle.

As a result of all this activity there was nothing in the house that hadn't, at some time or other, undergone his adaptations.

Nothing ever worked the way it was expected to for he had an odd way of re-modelling things with a contrary nature built in. Nell was terrified of electrical appliances as a result. If she switched something on and it refused to start, she considered herself lucky. Usually most things exploded into life to be as difficult as possible.

The self-propelling vacuum cleaner was one of his inventions. Prompted by Nell's constant nagging about the dust that all his objects harboured, he was driven to produce this invention, spending long nights in his workshop. The vacuum was an upright model with a dustbag hanging on a central pole and a foot which sucked up the dirt. When it emerged from the workshop the piece of equipment looked the same only there was a dial on the foot that could be switched round to set the machine at different speeds.

'It's entirely self-propelling. You don't have to walk about with it. You can set the dial to fast or slow and just leave it to get on with it.'

He smiled, delighted with his ingenuity. Nell grunted, not wanting to look up and see the thing that he held out towards her. She was sick of his peculiar ways, worn out by the knowledge that this 'toy' was supposed to placate her so that she wouldn't notice the cramped conditions. She resented the unfairness of their life at home, where he always had to be right and she had no say in what went on.

'Throw all your bloody junk out first and then I might be more appreciative,' she said sullenly and walked out of the room to sit on the stairs.

'I'll just put it in the cupboard,' he shouted up at her as he stowed it under the stairs.

She looked straight ahead pretending not to have seen him, and he went back into the kitchen while she sat out, not able to remain in that same room with him. The vacuum cleaner languished under the stairs. Nell stubbornly refused to use it. Each day he asked her if she had tried it out and she would stare blankly at him. 'Tried what out?

Eventually her curiosity got the better of her and she crept to the stair cupboard while he was out at work. She dragged the vacuum upstairs after her with difficulty because the base was solid metal and very heavy. She looked at it. It ran on batteries and there was a box on the side of the pole and a motor had been attached with wires coming from it. She didn't like the look of it at all, but making sure that the dial was at its lowest setting she flicked the switch on the arm. It gave off a low constant hum and a few gargles that must have terrified her. As it grew warm it began to trace large circles in the dust, moving in a great sweep. It was inefficient, slow and rhythmic.

Nell walked after it anxiously in case it bolted from her. She persuaded it to continue along the landing by pushing it and prodding it into the right direction, and thought, as her courage and confidence developed, that she would put it up to the next speed. She kicked the dial with her foot, but the disc slipped right round instead of resting in the second position and, with a noise like a motor bike revving up, it shot away from her travelling in ever increasing circles. It ricocheted off the narrow landing walls, taking chunks of plaster and wallpaper with it as it wrought its path of destruction like some demonic robot. It started to smoke and oily clouds spilled out as the motor grew red hot and emitted a smell like burnt hair.

Nell was terrified and ran behind it and, alternatively, in front of it when it suddenly changed direction and came full pelt towards her. She seized the top blanket from the bed behind her and charged at it, hoping to smother it and get to that dial before more smoke suffocated her. She was coughing and her eyes were streaming. But the vacuum sucked up part of the blanket and continued on its way, twisting it into a rope behind. At the head of the stairs it teetered for a minute then it plunged, taking pieces of carpet and wood from the banister with it. It crashed upside-down at the bottom, pouring out smoke and clouds of grey dust. The wallpaper hung in shreds. Nell raced down after it while it was immobilised and turned the switch into the 'off' position. There was a sighing noise as the bag collapsed like a sickly lung. And silence. Her sister came and helped her clean up.

'He's bloody mad that husband of yours. Bloody mad,' she said tying a damp cloth over her nose and mouth.

'Oh God it's awful. We'll choke,' Nell said, heaving a pail of water upstairs to wash the dust from the walls and floor where it covered everything as in a hundred years sleep.

But my brother and I thought he was funny.

Mother used to get her own back on my father whichever way

she could. He would bring something into the house and the next day she would stop the rag-and-bone man on his rounds and he'd take something off that mother had got out of the rooms while my father was at work. She disposed of a lot of his collection that way.

He never noticed or, if he did, he couldn't ask mother because she wasn't supposed to know what was there. And if he complained that he had mislaid something she would just say that it was a wonder he could find anything with all the rubbish he kept. Once he tried to make an inventory but he only got halfway through the first room and realised that it was hopeless. He couldn't keep a record of all the things that he had. And they were all necessary things that would come in handy.

'You never know when you might need one of these', he used to say.

There was no sudden change in the house, it continued much as it had always done for years. When Brendan was eleven, and news came that he had been awarded a scholarship to go to the Irish Christian Brothers' school, mother started to feel really desperate that he should have a room of his own.

Her breaking point arrived early one morning. She was standing at the front door with her sister, watching the cat climbing up the tree in the street, when a delivery van pulled up. Two men in boiler suits got out.

'2a Gwinter Street?' one asked. 'Here, love, sign this.'

Nell obediently signed while Margaret stared past her, horrified.

'Where shall we put it?' the two men asked, pushing a defunct shop-display fridge on a trolley between them.

'Back in the bloody van,' Nell said. 'That's not coming in here.'

The men stopped the fridge and leaned against it.

'Look, love, this is 2a Gwydir Street isn't it? This fridge was bought at auction by — where's the name?' and he rooted through his book.

'Yes, yes, yes,' Nell said. 'I don't doubt for one minute that my husband bought it . . . Tell me, how much did he give for it? she asked curiously.

'Er . . . let's have a look at that receipt. Four pounds eight and sixpence.'

'Four pounds eight and sixpence!' Margaret looked at Nell astounded. 'Oh Nell, and you haven't had a new coat for years and he's throwing money around like bloody Rockerfeller!'

'Well, what are we going to do with it?' the man asked.

'It's not coming in here — it won't get through the door.'

The man pointed with his thumb to the shop. 'I thought that's where it was going, not in your front room you know,' and they both laughed thinking that was a joke while Nell looked at Margaret and went white.

'The doors to that shop haven't been opened in years,' Margaret said trying to regain some calm while her sister became totally speechless.

'It's not a functioning shop, as you can see.'

The men looked worried.

'But it's got to go somewhere,' one said.

'Aye, back in the bloody van,' Nell uttered suddenly.

'It's all right,' the first man said coming back to them. 'I've measured the double doors of the shop. It'll go through. Can you open them up?'

The man did not know what he had asked. It was impossible. Her husband had sealed up all the windows and doors that winter, after Nell complained of draughts and she knew that the door was nailed up with slats of wood on the inside and behind it were stacks of God-alone-knew-what that would take weeks to shift. It was impenetrable.

'Er, me husband takes the keys with him to work,' she said lamely, too embarrassed to admit the truth.

'Well, we're not taking it back. We'll have to leave it on the pavement until you can get it inside,' he said tilting the fridge while his mate pushed it down from the back. It came to rest in front of the door.

'Oh that's all right,' Margaret said generously offering them the entire street. 'Just leave it right where it is.'

'Oh my God Margaret. What am I going to do now?' Nell asked as the men drove away.

'You're going to do nothing love, just nothing.'

That afternoon a constant stream of neighbours kept passing the house.

'Ere, 'es not going to open up as a butchers is 'e?' Mrs Daly asked. 'Only we've already got two, I don't think we need any more. You should warn him Mrs Mac. There'll be too much competition.'

Speculation was rife as to what was going on. Only my mother knew that this fridge signified nothing. It was simply another acquisition. But she couldn't tell that to the neighbours, not without arousing their pity. She spent the rest of the day hiding in the pantry and wouldn't answer the front door. Margaret went off in a hurry, saying that she had a plan. But she failed to return and when he came back from work the fridge was still sitting there.

He had to squeeze around it to let himself in. Nell said nothing and he looked at her quizically, waiting for her to complain. But she was determined to maintain her silence.

He had left specific instructions that it should be put in the yard and he was annoyed that it had just been dumped on the pavement.

'When was the fridge delivered?' he asked casually.

'What fridge?' she said.

'You mean that you haven't seen it! But it's right outside, in the street.'

'Oh. I haven't been out much today. I hadn't noticed.'

He looked at her but said nothing.

'Come to think of it there was a bit of a commotion earlier on. I saw a man running around with a measuring tape. He said something about one of our doors not being wide enough. I wondered what for. He wanted me to open the shop doors but I told him I couldn't. They're all boarded up on the inside, did you know that?'

He looked at his wife. Was it true then, he wondered, that the backyard door was too narrow. He had checked it. Or he thought that he had. He got up thoughtfully and went towards his shop and came back clutching a metal ruler. Without a word to Nell, he went onto the street and started measuring.

'What's if for then? Mr McGloughlan asked him.

'Oh nothing in particular,' he said, preoccupied with measuring.

They were right! He had forgotten to measure the rubber runners on the fridge which added nearly two inches to the width. The doorframe was just too narrow. What could he do? He was a man who prided himself on his ability to solve problems.

'How are you going to move it?' Mr McGloughlan got no reply. My father had already gone back indoors to sit at the table and draw diagrams of pulleys.

There was a loud knock at the door and my mother ushered a policeman into the room.

'Does that fridge belong to you?' he asked brusquely, pointing through the window into the street.

'Yes officer, it does,' faltered my father, rather taken aback by an officer of the law. He hoped no one had seen him arrive, but he knew that they must have. He was growing hot around the ears. His neck always went red when he was angry, now there was a rosy flush spreading up the back of it.

'As an officer of the law I am to warn you that it is causing an obstruction on a public right of way and I request that you move it immediately. I've had one complaint already and I came round earlier to look for myself. This thing has been sitting out on the street all day.'

'Yes, well officer, you see I'm just in from work.'

'I know. The person who reported it said that you wouldn't be back until seven. I understand that your wife was unable to open doors that had been sealed up. This could be a serious fire hazard.'

My father's face went crimson. What else did this man know?

'Look, you've got three hours to shift that thing. I'll be back this way at ten o'clock tonight and if I see it still out there, I'll be seeing you in court.'

Nell went on drinking her tea as if nothing was happening. She was to do nothing.

'You'll have to help me,' he shouted, forgetting his well thought out pulley in the first rush of panic. He paced up and down.

Nell was darning a sock. 'Help you what?'

'To move the bloody fridge. Didn't you hear what the policeman said?'

'Oh that,' she said slowly and infuriatingly. 'I heard'. She didn't move.

He went backwards and forwards with an assortment of tools. She heard banging and crashing and the sound of wood splintering. Eventually her curiosity got the better of her. She went out into the yard and saw that he had removed the entire back door, and hacked away at the doorjamb so that it hung in splinters.

'Help me to shift this bloody fridge!' he yelled, seeing her standing by the step with a sock in her hand.

'I don't want that thing in the house. We're full up with junk and you've got to bring more home. There must be something the matter with you.'

'It's you there's something wrong with. Other wives help their husbands. What do I get? Bloody complaints all the time. Now, give me a hand.'

Nell didn't know what possessed her, but the sound of him giving her an order made her obstinate.

'Don't you ever talk to me like that again. If you think I would help you to bring more bloody junk into this house you must be away in the head.'

She looked over the street to where the neighbours were gathering having heard all the shouting and hammering, and quickly turned her back.

'Come on Mac, we'll give you a hand to shift it.'

It took four men and my father to lift and carry the thing. They pushed it through the door which was only a brick frame now, and half way through it jammed. Mother was out in a flash, back in the yard shouting, not caring who knew.

'You can't leave it there!' You're not bringing it in here you miserable swine!'

The men looked shocked.

'This is the help I get from my wife,' Bill started saying, hoping to shut her up and show what an unreasonable wife he had to put up with. They looked embarrassed. Normally Nell would have retreated, but this time she had been pushed beyond endurance.

'And this is what I get, a bloody refrigerator stuck in the doorway. You don't know what I've had to put up with!' she shouted to the neighbours over the street. 'Every room is packed with rubbish that he keeps bringing home . . . '

'Get back inside,' my father said fiercely.

'Don't think you can give me orders mate!' she snapped at him. 'You've ruined my life enough as it is. Do you know that we all sleep in the same room because — you see those rooms up there?' The heads all looked up while my mother pointed from the yard. 'Those rooms up there are all full of junk that this man has brought in, and the parlour is full too. We live in two pokey rooms and the house is full of things like this . . . this . . . ' but she could not think of a word strong enough, so she kicked the fridge with her foot angrily and went back inside, sobbing hysterically.

In the front room she looked at her face in the mirror and hated herself. What had she done? She was a fool, she had let the story out after years of bottling it up. She was like a robot as she took her hat and coat.

'Get your things,' she said to Brendan and me. 'We're not staying here tonight.'

We walked out of the house and down the street to Aunt Margaret's.

'Never mind Nell,' she said. 'You had to say all that.'

'Oh God, how can I ever go back there?' my mother sobbed. 'Everyone knows.'

'Aye they all know the sort of man you are married to. It's no reflection on you. There's nothing wrong in wanting a decent home for your kids, there's nothing you need to be ashamed of. He's the one that's being selfish. He forced you to that showdown. He had it coming. And anyway, I've got an idea.'

Margaret smiled her crafty look as she poured out more tea. 'You could do very well out of this.'

The next morning, back at home, my mother and my aunt stood out in the yard looking at the fridge that stood squarely in place. My father must have worked half the night with ropes and pulleys, for it was encased in a weblike construction of old washing lines, and it had obviously been lowered down over the wall.

'That's determination for you,' my aunt said, and I think that was the only time I ever heard her say anything that approached admiration for him. 'Now Nell, you're got to be as determined. You've allowed all this to go on for long enough.'

'But I'll never get this out. It's here to stay.'

'All right. So it's here to stay, until he sees reason. But the rest of the house doesn't have to wait for him now, does it?'

My mother looked at her sister, and squared her shoulders.

'Let's find a pen. You can help me word the advert.'

For the following two weeks there seemed to be a constant parade of visitors who all came in the morning, shuffled about upstairs and left quite quickly carrying parcels and shopping bags. They were mostly men who talked about 'the business', between themselves. Every evening, before my father came home, Margaret ran about squirting fly spray so that the entire house reeked of it.

'Does she have to do that?' my father asked one night, catching her running along the landing.

'Oh there are so many flies about now,' my mother said pouring scent onto herself.

'You know, I'm sure that I can smell tobacco smoke,' he said sniffing.

'I think it's the fly spray, bit strong isn't it?'

Although Brendan and I didn't know what was going on, we knew that we were under close guard and that we were not to ask any questions or say anything to father.

My mother had taken out an advert in a trade paper, announcing the total liquidation of stock for a quick sale and scrap dealers had turned up during the hours that she had specified. The neighbours had all been warned if they saw anything odd they were not to mention it to Mac.

'It's a surprise,' mother said smiling.

There was a wall of silence surrounding the entire activity.

Two weeks from when the fridge had first dropped in and had given Margaret the idea, she stood with her sister in the completely empty room upstairs. They had shifted odd things themselves. Margaret had taken things that even the scrap dealers didn't want and had hidden them in her coal cellar. There was only a bag of rusted tins and some bits of hosepipe left, and some picture frames. Margaret took care of those.

Nell spread her arms out and turned a circle. 'Look at it Margaret.'

For the first time in the house she could move without knocking into something.

'How much did we make?'

'Thirty-four pounds, eight shillings.'

'More than enough to get it decorated and get curtains and lino. Oh Margaret!'

'Come on,' said the other. 'Let's start getting the dust up.'

Both women worked with fury and passion, scrubbing the bare boards and washing all the surfaces, getting everything ready to paint. And every evening Nell locked the door and hung the grey key back up by the mantelpiece. She felt as if the weight of all that paraphenalia had been lifted from her. And she sailed about singing.

Of course Nell knew that the time would come when he would discover it. It happened one night, shortly after he came home from work, he took the key and went upstairs. Nell felt herself growing hot. She put down her sewing and strained to hear. He might not go into that room . . . but she heard his footsteps directly overhead. They stopped short. She could only imagine his face. She heard the door bang against the wall, heard him running downstairs. He was frantic. He grabbed his coat and hat.

'Nell! Nell! check that the kids are all right. I'm going to the police station!'

'What in the name of God for?'

'We've been burgled!' he said, as he ran off up the road.

My father drove them all mad at the police station.

'What exactly has been taken?' they asked and he pulled out his incomplete inventory and explained that it was only part of the loss.

'Well that's a great start,' said the sergeant, taking the list from him. But as he read down his face changed.

'Are you having me on or what?' he said, passing the paper to the deputy officer.

The list must have seemed odd.

Item 1: 58 radio valves in wooden container. Defunct.

Item 2: 6 pairs binoculars. Non-functional.

Item 3: 4 lenses from lighthouse . . . and so on down the paper.

'Look mate, er what about things like furniture? You know, table, chairs. You said it was an upstairs bedroom they got into. Did they leave the bed or what?'

'They've completely stripped it out. It's empty, empty,' said my father his head in his hands, unable to understand why they did not see the great loss that mankind had suffered by this theft.

'Completely stripped it out eh? Does that mean that the bed was taken then?'

'Oh no. There was no bed in it.'

'No bed hmmm. Er, was there any furniture at all then?'

'Oh yes,' he said turning the list over. 'Look here's all the furniture itemised. Well, most of it.'

And there, on the opposite page, was a series of groups:

Item 78: 3 cane-backed chairs to be re-caned.

Item 79: one teak chest without lid.

Item 80: one nest of tables — 3 legs missing in all . . . and so on.

'Look mate. What the hell are you, a factory or something?'

My poor father was too upset to even notice the tone creeping into their voices.

'Here,' said the officer, 'didn't we have some trouble from you just recently? What's that address, 2a Gwinter Street? Here officer, remember I said there was a great big fridge out on the street?

Obstruction that's what we nearly had you for. Get it shifted then?'

My father started to explain proudly how we owed a great deal to the ancient Egyptians.

'Well Officer McNulty, as you seem to know so much about this case . . . ' the sergeant interrupted, 'I suggest you go round and investigate.'

'Thanks sarge, I'll do the same for you some time.'

The policeman was led upstairs and into the room, where he saw my mother and my aunt up ladders paperhanging.

'Oh hello dear,' my mother said rather too brightly. 'We thought we'd start on Brendan's room and surprise you. It's going to look nice, isn't it?

'Good evening officer,' said Margaret. 'Anything the matter?'

'Have you seen anything strange lately?' he asked. 'Only you're supposed to have been burgled.'

'Well apart from a fridge practically coming through the roof — oh, and we've got no back door now, but my husband knocked that in with a hatchet. No, I can't say I've noticed anything peculiar.'

'Where exactly is the fridge now?'

'It's out in the backyard'

'Handy is it? Keep your coal in it?'

'Oh it's nothing to do with me. My husband makes all the decisions.'

'Right,' he said surveying the scene. 'You don't mind if I go out and take a look at it do you?'

Out in the yard father was already standing over the fridge muttering. 'What is going on?' he kept repeating.'What is going on?' and out of the body of the fridge he lifted a plastic sack full of rusted tins of paint and some bits of hosepipe.

'Officer,' he said, seeing the man approach. 'I've recovered some of the items.'

'Oh, he forgets things all the time, don't you Bill?' my mother said having followed the policeman down while Margaret whispered in an undertone to the man — 'He gets very confused, very confused . . . sees things, you know, and has the odd moment when he goes a bit berserk. She told you about the hatchet didn't she? Very odd that was, and unprovoked too.'

'Well,' said the policeman writing down in his book. 'I'll say that some of the items have been recovered, and we'll keep an eye out for the rest or for anything suspicious. Most probably an organised gang with a van.'

He hoped that he sounded sincere as he tried to slip out through the hole in the wall where the door had been. He didn't see that he had any choice but to try and bluff his way out. He hated domestic affairs, and there was something very odd about that family anyway. That poor man, he was obviously deluded. And those poor women, he thought, having to deal with him day in day out. There was no doubt about it, some people deserved medals, they were the salt of the earth. Ordinary folk looking after their own. He knew that he would have to file some sort of a report. How he would begin writing it he just couldn't say. Oh the job certainly had it's drawbacks. Why hadn't they warned him when he was still a cadet?

'A van!' my father said. 'That's it! They'd need a van. Didn't you say that there was a van here the day they brought the fridge? They parked the van here didn't they? And now look, the stuff starts turning up in the fridge. They must have been stripping the place while the feller was diverting you. What a gang of crooks! That's these quick sale auctions for you!'

'Oh, you mean that you didn't order the van? And I really believed that you were clearing the room out at last.'

'Some people never change do they?' Margaret said sadly.

'I mean . . . ' my mother continued, getting into her stride, 'I've been waiting for you twelve years now. I'm beginning to feel that you've no intention of getting these rooms ready. Like that shop . . . '

That was a good angle. Margaret had told her to get that in at all costs. She winked at her sister.

'The policeman said that it was a fire hazard, all that stuff. You can't get the doors open can you?' Margaret reminded her sister.

'Oh yes, that's right. Look, should I call that young feller back and ask what we can do about it? I mean, we might need some sort of insurance . . . '

'Now, now,' said my father.' I don't think that's necessary.'

'By the time he had finished talking he'd admitted that it was always his intention to clear the room out and Margaret let him save face by believing that he had given instructions and then forgotten.

'Oh you're such a busy man,' she said. 'You've got so much on you mind.'

Who knows, he may have even believed it himself by the time they had finished with him.

In the yard were tied up bundles of newspaper waiting for the binman. Suddenly father's eye caught something. On the top of one of the piles was a funny little paper, half the size of the *Echo*.

'What's that? he asked and his eye caught the words 'A quick sale. Everything for under ten shillings. Bring your own transport. No deliveries undertaken.'

'At least they can't be crooks,' he said laughing.

'I wouldn't upset yourself anymore,' Margaret said. 'You've had a shock, and you've been working too hard. Take him in Nell and get him a good strong cup of tea.'

As he sat in the front room, drinking from one of the best cups, he wondered if maybe he had been a little too hard on his wife's sister in the past. He was seeing another side to her personality. She was no fool, he thought.

And he was right. Out in the yard Margaret had quickly shredded the piece of paper thinking that she would have to show Nell how to cover her tracks more carefully.

I wonder if it was about this time that he moved into the cellar. Perhaps he had known about it since the start, but as the other rooms became empty some of the junk must have been deposited there. We should have know that it was all too precious for him to just throw out.

The year after he died my mother was sorting through the piles of rubbish in his workshop, for the shop remained my father's hideout even when the rest of the house had long returned to its original function. The workshop remained packed from floor to ceiling, the doors always sealed from behind. She pulled up some rotten lino to throw out and found the trap door. Curiously she had pulled it open. Grating on its rusted hinges, it swung back. She peered down into the dark space beneath her to discover the underground world that had been my father's.

It was packed solid. We heard her shouting hysterically for us to bring a flashlight and we ran to see her head appearing from the floor.

'Come down here! Come down here!' she was yelling.

Brendan threw a beam of light down the shaft and we saw my mother standing surrounded by huge shapes, walled in like the Egyptians for whom Father had so much respect.

'Look at this!' she shrieked as the light bounced off the unrecognisable objects. 'I can't believe it! I can't believe it!'

I never knew if she was crying with rage or delight. For she must have realised that she had just discovered the finest monument her husband could have wished for.

The Coat

There were always gangs of kids then, out on the streets playing. You had only to go out of your front door to become swept up in some eternal game. And you played out until it was dark. Only when you could no longer see the ball to catch it, or the features of your companions' faces as they stood in front of you obscured by shadows, only then was it time to call an end.

The only interruptions were mothers needing their children to go for errands.

'Come here and run a message,' they shouted from doorways and a child obliged with an ill grace, dragged away from the sport.

Kids brought bread and jam with them and sat out on steps to eat, not wanting to miss anything that happened.

There were always dogs that roamed without collar or lead. But they were not strays. Strays were strangers that the other dogs immediately turned on, but these dogs all had owners and were known to us. They never went far, seldom got lost, and it was rare when any of them failed to come home. For, like us, they knew their territory which had been fought over and was clearly drawn out as they nosed their routes, scenting their way through the back entries where the stale rubbish filled the air. Down behind the chip shop, where the discarded vertibrae of fillets collected into a temporary graveyard that reeked of salt-fish, they skirted the puddles of black grease, leaving those to the birds who scratched marks across their gelling surface.

And there were always cats, eyes luminous from dark doorways; backs bunched and bristling, hissing at dogs. Behind McCawleys the Butcher's the entry took on the smell of dried blood mingled with sawdust which, every day, saw the prize fight of mongrels for some ossified trophy.

Even with my eyes shut I could tell exactly where I was. The greengrocer's smelt of three-day-old cabbage, the leaves turned to jelly, while the stalks and shoots lined the outside walls in sacks. There were rotting marrows and large pulpy vegetables that changed shape as their walls collapsed. Here was the decay of living matter.

Despite this it was only in my seventh summer that I ever saw a rat, running between a neighbour's house. It ran into Old Mrs Daly's backyard where the miracle had happened years before. I was terrified but excited and ran with my small friend yelling 'Rat! Rat!' swollen with the importance of our news. Out on the street a huddle of neighbours swiftly encircled us as we knocked triumphantly on Mrs Daly's front door. Her eyes were suspicious and she talked over our heads to the adults as though we were not there.

'Well, that's mighty peculiar — mighty peculiar indeed.'

'It is odd isn't it?' they all agreed. Her eyes flickered on us for an instant.

'Are you sure it was a rat?' 'How do you know it was?' 'What did it look like?' 'It sounds mightly suspicious to me, mightly suspicious indeed,' Mrs Daly said, folding her arms across her chest. She did not have a rat, none of the neighbours did.

'They're just a couple of kids,' one old man said.

'They're just playing, love,' Mrs Lawson reassured her.

We walked away with as much affronted dignity as we could possess.

'Well I hope it bloody bites her!' my mother said after I had told her the story. We kept our cat in for a week. 'Rats are vicious — I'm not having our Tiddle poisoned by someone else's, not after they've been warned.'

My friend's parents likewise incarcerated their ginger tom in the outside lavatory every night.

'Let her sort her own bloody rat out if she can't even take your word,' her father said. It was a serious offence to doubt someone'e integrity.

When we were forced to attend school for the first time it broke up our routine and I remember how the evenings were suddenly cut short by winter, leaving us no time to play on the streets. But the following summer granted us a reprieve, a return to our old ways. Unknown to us we had grown older, but we only felt that the games lacked meaning.

One of our favourite pastimes had been to watch the deliveries to the corner shop, for each day brought new consignments. Crowds of children would gather, sitting on the cold stone mounts around the bay windows that Mrs Furlong blamed Hitler for.

'That bloody get! I'd still have me railings if it weren't for him!

Many of the women felt the same way as they cleared up after the dogs that always found their way in to the sheltered bit of the bay window. But the mounts provided first class viewing facilities for the pastry van spectacle. It was really the delivery boy that we looked out for, smart in his white apron with crates piled up on his head. We were always waiting for the trip that would send the pies and loaves scattering along a pavement rich in messages and chalky hopscotch numbers. Although we relished the prospect of such an accident, it never happened.

Once, egged on by the rest of us, a slow boy that none of us wanted to play with, called after him, "Ey Mister! Is dem trays glued to yer 'at?' and the delivery boy had looked shiftily from the corner of his eyes, unable to turn his head pinioned to his cargo.

'Gawan! Clear off the lot of yous!' he shouted and we raced away, terrified in case he should throw his burden to the ground and give chase.

For days after, the poor lump thought he was a hero.

'I did it . . . I asked 'im!' he repeated whenever we saw him, reliving his one glorious moment. But it bored us, even seemed a rather silly thing to have done, and the idea of waiting day after day for a repeat performance depressed us. We were slowly moving on, turning away from old games.

My eighth and ninth summers gave way to playing with the girls. We decided that boys were stupid and showed off all the time, and besides we could not see any point in them. We wanted to grow up, we were in a hurry to be women. We sat around on doorsteps imagining ourselves as we would like to be. It soon became a favourite game.

'What are you wearing? What are you wearing? we asked each other as we each held a vision of ourselves in the future.

'A green coat with a cherry red cravat,' said Siobhan.

'White boots and a black polo neck jumper,' said Eileen.

'A camel coat,' I said remembering a woman I had once seen at mass who wore a coat of that description and carried a brown bag. That would be me in ten years.

To us then, clothes were passports into different worlds. They epitomised the people we would become. Once we were dressed a certain way we would be like snakes shedding skins for we would obliterate our past, removing our history like an overcoat to emerge poised and confident. Magazine women. I would wear my hair swept up in a french roll like my eldest cousin, and a pair of diamante clip earrings. I would let my finger nails grow and paint them dark red and live in a dust free home that would be painted all white, with white carpets and fitted cupboards. There would be no hard corners or ugly pieces of furniture. Everything would be in its rightful place, like the display bedroom in Lewis's window down town.

If anyone from our street went on holiday they always bought something new to wear. No one wanted to open a suitcase full of the smells of home in a bed and breakfast. They wanted to put on something unblemished, so that they could assume the role of someone else for a week. Even hospital meant a new pair of pyjamas.

'You can't be making a show of me in those rotten things,' mothers shouted at their sick children, nervous in case the world discovered their secrets. Socks held up with bits of string, safety pins holding seams together, elastic worn and frayed, but all kept furtively out of sight.

'I'd like a pair of shiny patent leather boots and a straight shift dress,' said Brigid.

'Oh. I've got one of those,' Kirstie announced. 'It's navy blue with a white anchor on the front — mam bought it down town.'

She stood up, brushing the dust off her skirt and began to walk away. She had almost reached the corner when she stopped, remembering something she had still to tell us, she turned back 'And I've got a matching bag,' she shouted over her shoulder before disappearing from sight.

We were all a bit wary of Kirstie. Not only were both of her parents English, but her grandparents were also, both sets. There was no Irish ancestry at all. I did not understand how this was possible. And she had more than one pair of shoes. She even had a pair, it was rumoured, that had been bought specially just to match her coat. I had never heard of such a thing before. It seemed an extreme of luxury, which I vowed I would adopt when I was an adult and had money to spend.

I was in Kirstie's house one day when her mother produced a

map of Europe and, like a child, traced around the coast with her finger.

'We've been all the way around here,' and she drew her finger down to Cornwall, 'and all the way up here, and up this side,' and she smiled in a self satisfied way while Kirstie took her turn tracing the same route aping her mother.

'I've been here, and all along here,' she slowly moved her square bitten nail laboriously up the coast, drawing out the place names that she could read to make them last longer. 'And . . .er . . . have I been there?'

'No, no that's not England — but you've been here . . . ,' and the mother guided the child's slow hands.

'This is where we're going on holiday. Where are you going?'

'I don't know,' I said, 'I'm not sure.'

Then Kirstie chimed in, 'You never go on holiday. You never do. You never go on holiday.' She began to turn it into a little song while I stood feeling awkward. Suddenly she snatched the map from her mother's grasp and forced my hand onto the page and a strange triumphant look came into her eyes. 'Tell us where you've been, go on, show us.'

I stared blankly at the map, embarrassed. I knew that I was lacking in something, or that I had done something wrong, for there was nowhere I could claim to have visited.

'Tell your friend about your holiday in Wales,' said her mother, pleased with herself for raising a superior child that was not awkward when asked questions and knew how to converse on matters of general interest.

Look, show your friend where it is on the map,' she said leaving us and Kirstie told me about the holiday she had been on in Wales, in a caravan.

'We met a family from the south of England, probably London, yes I'm sure it was because they knew the Queen, and they spoke proper English like on the telly. So did my parents,' she added hastily, 'for the whole week that we were away. And I said 'Yessssss,' she drew out the hissing noise at the end of the word, letting me hear that she could speak correctly when she wanted.

'They had a car, a green one. Their son Mark was the same age as me, only taller.'

I looked at her enviously. Their son Mark became the idealised male not at all like the boys I knew who hung about with us in groups. She had been wearing her navy shift dress when they had met.

One day shortly after the geography lesson I was sitting out playing with the others.

'I want a red beret with a matching red bolero jacket and white fur trimming, and I want a red skating skirt, then I'll be an ice skater and go skating on Sefton Park lake when it freezes,' said Eileen.

We closed our eyes whirling around to the ice dance in our heads.

'And I'll come and watch you in my camel coat,' I said seeing myself wrapped up warmly, surrounded by people in fur hats as the park boating lake became a winter palace.

Kirstie tilted her head back and surveyed us along the length of her nose. 'What difference does it make what you wear?' She arched her eyebrows and tried unsuccessfully to curb a gleeful smile by puckering her mouth in an attempt to appear grown up while she made the observation. 'You never go anywhere', and turned to direct her gaze upon me. 'Do you think anybody is going to look at you? Who on earth do you expect to meet here?'

I felt that once again I had done something terribly wrong by dreaming out of bounds. I had never left our street yet I was daring to play imaginary games with myself in a leading role. Kirstie reminded me that I had no right to expect anything. But it was not this that stopped me playing, although none of us had the heart to for a while after. But for me, something of a diversion occurred.

My mother's cousin, Hannah came to stay for a weekend. We called her Aunt Hannah out of politeness but we did not see her often enough to call her 'auntie'. I remember how she looked the day she arrived. Her light brown hair was cut short and permanently waved. I knew that she would never have gone out in curlers, in fact I doubted if she ever wore them, although she did wear make up, but on her it looked normal. I supposed that she wore it all the time, even when she was doing the housework and that she always looked well dressed, unlike my mother who wore the same colourless skirt and cardigan day after day. She had on a well tailored bluish two piece with a narrow nipped-in-the-waist jacket with a velvet collar, and she carried a black shiny clutch bag. To me she seemed the right sort of person to wear a camel coat.

On Saturday Hannah wanted to shop so we were to go into town where the large department stores were. I was hardly ever taken into town with the adults so it was a big event for me. It was to be a special day out shopping and even mother was making an effort, caught up in Hannah's glow. She sponged down her coat the night before trying to remove as many stains as she could, and dug out a pair of good earrings that had once belonged to grandmother.

'You really ought to make the best of yourself, Leah,' Hannah encouraged. 'Here, try some of this lipstick.' But mother looked clownish and dressed up with a vermilion mouth.

'I don't think it's me,' and she started to wipe it away.

'No, no, It just takes some getting used to, you have to make an effort first.'

Father grimaced and walked out the door. He stood for a few minutes on the paving not knowing what to do, then just as oddly came back indoors and started dragging planks of wood out of the loft, leaving trails of wood everywhere. My father hated the fuss mother made whenever Hannah was to come. 'Oh I see royalty's coming,' he'd say surveying the white tablecloth and the plates of sandwiches. He would take himself off to his workshop.

This time he was visibly disturbed.

'Oh Jesus! Let's get out!' my mother said, rolling her eyes heaven-ward as her husband began turning the only room into a woodyard.

Hannah wore a felt cartwheel hat that matched her suit, and a little cape of silver fur that hung around her shoulders and clasped with a delicate chain around her throat. Her shoes were well heeled and shiny. I hoped that we had been noticed leaving the house. I felt proud to be seen with her, as if some of Hannah's glamour rubbed off onto me. I never thought that the contrast between us could just as likely work to our disadvantage as we trailed along behind. It was like escaping. We walked around the city centre in and out of the big shops looking at silk scarves and fancy bottles of perfumes.

Aunt Hannah glided in and out with a nonchalance that astounded and struck fear into my mother. It was as if she had an undeniable right to be where ever she was, the unhurried way she approached a counter, demanding to know the cost of everything. Holding material up to the light while her expert fingers felt the quality between them. All the world seemed to be at Aunt Hannah's disposal, to be given her approval, wrapped up and taken home. She could walk away without flinching after engaging sales staff in conversation about a particular commodity that she then dismissed; 'I'll leave it thank you,' was all she needed to say before turning on her smart heels.

On my rare excursions into town with my mother I was rendered helpless by repeated warnings. 'Don't touch!' 'Leave that!' I was powerless to choose, examine or criticise. Everytime a sales assistant approached us my mother would stammer and blush. 'I'm only looking,' she would say defensively, dropping the article back onto the counter and tripping over on her weak ankle in her haste to get out of the store.

But with Hannah it was. 'Smell this scent.' 'Try this soap.' 'Feel this fabric.' 'Taste this cheese.' Nobody could rush Hannah.

My mother stood uneasily shifting from one foot to the other as her cousin coolly ran her hand over the furs that were chained onto a rack. 'Come away Hannah,' she hissed urgently in an undertone so that the store detectives would not hear her. 'They know we're not going to buy anything.'

She suddenly became rigid and stood to attention as the colour drained from her face.

'Whatever's the matter Leah?'

My mother was staring straight ahead as if hypnotised. Aunt Hannah and I exchanged glances — maybe she was ill. A low seated growl emerged from mother's throat. It sounded barely human. Maybe she was going to have a convulsion right there among all the fur coats. She pointed with her finger, so furtively that it struck me she had possibly lost control of all but this part of her body, a victim of sudden paralysis. My grandmother had suffered a stroke they told me, before I was born, leaving her lopsided, unable to move half of her face. The finger directed us to look in a mirror where we stared at our perplexed faces and mother in her reflected trauma.

'What on earth . . . ?' Hannah began, to be cut off by mother whispering 'Camera, camera.' We looked helplessly at each other 'They're filming me for the police station.'

Hannah exploded into laughter . 'Well just you be careful and don't be leaving fingerprints!' she said, turning back to continue her search and leaving mother in the grip of the electronic eye that she had heard about from a neighbour. She was certain that she had seen a shadow move in the glass which proved beyond doubt that it was two-way. And she had been told about hidden cameras. Some of the big shops did have them.

'Oh look, Leah, this little musquash is lovely,' said Hannah trying to draw her out from her catatonic state while in the background the assistants began to gather. Soon they would close in on us, their crimson nails twitching. Singly they advanced, dressed in black skirts and white blouses, like clerics with all hair dragged severely away from their pale powdered faces.

'Can I help Modom?'

Mother was already white with fear and sinking lower between the clothes racks. Soon she would be on her knees.

'Would you like any assistance?'

'Which model is Modom looking for?'

'Is there a particular style, or length?'

'Would you like to try one on?'

I felt a sharp pain in my left shoulder. Turning round I saw the glazed eyes of my mother who had unconsciously reached out and gripped me tightly to stop herself from fainting as she watched Hannah slip on the coat.

'The fool, the fool!' she repeated in horror. 'Holy Mary, Mother of God! Deliver us from this! ' she prayed, beside herself with fright.

'What do you think, Leah?' Hannah asked, turning round in front of a mirror and trying to look at her back. From behind me came the sound of spluttering as Mother tried, struggled, to regain the use of her tongue. Hannah was calmly asking the price.

'No. I don't think that its the right number for me . . . doesn't do a thing for me really. Thanks,' and she dropped it off her shoulders waiting for an assistant to help her out of it.

'Good day,' she smiled charmingly, and taking Mother by the elbow led her out firmly towards the lift.

Out in the street Mother made a swift recovery and strode off purposefully in the direction of Woolworth's. She led us to the cafeteria on the third floor.

'It'll steady me nerves having a cup of tea, she whispered to me as we drew near on the escalator. We could already hear the clatter and rattle of crockery before we drew up level with the floor. It was as if all manner of eating implements were being thrown down on to the tables, for everything crashed into place while some knives and forks skidded off metal topped tables and landed on the floor to be picked up and wiped on someone's jumper to be used again. The metal of the tables, once shiny, was now scratched and dull through repeated use. But no matter how worn the tops, they were still cold and unwelcoming. Their lived-in look was of the nature of having been swiftly evacuated.

Inside people coughed and smoked and there was a fishy odour lingering from the previous day that hung on everything. Girls in greasy nylon overalls were pushing the trolleys between the aisles with stacks of dirty plates that shook perilously as they rattled along. Each trolley had a bowl of grey soapy water which slopped over the sides as they rattled from one end of the cafeteria to the other. The girls cleared the tables and emptied the ash trays using the same cloth they wiped the tables with to give the ashtrays a polish, and wringing them out in the bowl. There was an endless· queue of people around the self-service counter surveying the warmed up food.

I knew the place already having been occasionally taken there as a treat.

Hannah's face dropped. 'Is there nowhere quieter?' she asked, while my mother stared blankly at her.

'They're all the same.'

'No they're not.' She took her place in the queue. 'It's nice to be able to relax occasionally, but in these places everyone is so tired and overworked that you are made to feel that you are in the way. Look around, there isn't a smiling face behind this counter, and I don't blame them. And those poor little girls out there on the floor, they're told to clean the tables while the customers are still eating. It makes me want to hurry all the time so that I don't become a nuisance to them. But remember that you are paying to sit here so why should you have to feel as though you have done something wrong? These places are supposed to serve the public after all, not antagonise them.'

Aunt Hannah's philosophy was that everything was for her use. The world was hers, services existed for her good, while my poor mother battled against everything, trying not to say the wrong thing, be in the wrong place, or demand more than her due. To us it was normal to expect to be jostled out of the way, treated to surly comments and made to feel awkward. Somehow we had learnt that this was what we deserved. Were we truly the meek inheriting the earth?

Later we were walking down Bold Street when I saw it. In the window. A camel coat with brown revers. I stopped and looked at it. It had deep square pockets which the dummy's hands were thrust into. It was roomy and had been pinned up at the back as if caught in a gust of wind, and the child model laughed, positioned amongst paper leaves, walking with a black toy dog. That was exactly what I wanted to be, walking down a leafy lane in my camel jacket.

'Come on,' Mother said. 'There's no point looking at things you can't have.'

Hannah opened her mouth as if to say something, but stopped. 'Come on,' she said, 'or we'll miss the bus. It's nice though isn't it?' looking back towards the window.

I decided there and then that I was going to be like Hannah when I grew up — scared of nothing.

Ten days after Hannah's departure a parcel arrived addressed to mother. It was large, lumpy and mysterious in it's brown paper and string.

'Well let me put the shopping away and take me coat off first,' she said matter-of-factly when she came in through the door and I flung myself at her breathlessly.

'Mum, Look! There's a parcel for you. It came earlier when you were out!'

Parcels never arrived at our house, but for what seemed an age mother put tins inside the larder taking longer over it than usual. Even father was agitated. 'I'll finish that,' he said pulling paper bags out of her shopper.

'Don't rush me.' She intended to savour the suspense the parcel was generating. She approached the sideboard, where it had been left, cautiously, as if the parcel might explode in her face. She ran her hands over it.

'There's no address of the sender,' and looking puzzled she turned it over to inspect it. Slowly she began to untie the string, laboriously unravelling knots with her fingers, spending five minutes on each one, her face content. I hardly dared breathe while she eked out her surprise.

She drew out a pair of leather gloves from the top of the package. 'Hannah!' she said reproachfully. But her face softened as she unfolded the paper back revealing the camel jacket. She held it up to me. 'Come and try it on, and remember, it's for Sundays.'

All week the jacket hung in my parents' wardrobe that perfumed the air with mothballs whenever the heavy mirrored door creaked open. I kept stealing in to look at the jacket and I would slip my hand under the dust sheet to feel its warm softness.

I thought that Sunday would never come. I longed to go to Mass with a fervour that was uncommon, all to be seen in my new jacket. But the next Sunday did not bring about my hopes.

'You're not wearing it now and that's final. It's far too hot to be wearing a camel jacket.'

I began to cry knowing that I would probably not live until the autumn if I could not wear the coat before then. Then they would be sorry, with the camel jacket wasted, with me dead. Maybe they would let me be buried in it. Tears poured down my cheeks.

'Why can't I wear it?'

'Because I say so!' My mother the tyrant.

And so Mass was torture, my eyes red and puffy. And I was ashamed, feeling everyone's stare upon me. I could not go to communion and let everyone see my face which I was keeping piously bowed. When father nudged me for the offertory I did not move.

'I'm not going,' I mouthed as he stood back in the aisle for me insensitively.

I spent all Sunday in tears. My object of desire had caused me to neglect God. Life would be intolerable unless I could do something.

The following day, when mother was out and father busy sawing wood in the yard, I crept into the bedroom and took the jacket off the hanger carefully peeling back the polythene bag to stop it rustling and covering the jacket with my old school mac I raced out towards the front door leaving the navy blue gabardine in the hall. Once out of the house I slipped on the jacket. The sleeves were a bit too long. Undaunted I rolled them back. I walked to the next street trying to catch a glimpse of myself in the windows as I went past. Nobody seemed to notice. When I saw a group of my friends over by one of the stone mounts I walked towards them, forcing myself to slow down so that I might make the right impression.

'Is that it then?' Eileen asked. 'It's lovely.'

'Yeah,' I said proudly, 'this is it,' and made to sit down but stopped. I could not risk getting it dirty. I stood there awkwardly. They were all in tee-shirts and shorts. I began to feel uncomfortably hot.

'I want a matching beach set, towelling, like the girl on the telly.'

'And I want a sun tan,' said Siobhan, lifting her pale stick-like arms out towards the sun. 'Then I will lie by a swimming pool, New Brighton, blue sky and the open sea.'

I felt terribly warm. Winter was out it seemed and summer definitely in.

'I wonder what it's like to water ski?'

'Or to go to a beach party?'

It was our perspiring red-bricked summer that left me stranded in my jacket unable to swim.

But then the very worst thing that could have happened did happen. My mother saw me. I had not thought to hide myself, because I was sure that she would never recognise me, so cool, poised and confident I would have become. But she came straight across the road with real anger on her face. I hated that look of hers.

'I'll murder you!' she shrieked, bringing the flat of her hand down over my ear. 'Your father will kill you when I tell him!' and in front of everyone I was dragged home crying, the coat and cause of all my suffering hanging limply around me.

'Get inside and take that off!'

My friends had shrunk into a tiny huddle watching helplessly as I was snatched away. I knew that they were feeling sorry for me, but this was not how I had imagined it. This was not the effect that I had wanted to create.

I noticed how the streets all stayed the same. There were no leafy lanes, and the same dogs sniffed at the same dustbins. The delivery boy did not choose that day to slip and I was unchanged. The dark corners of the kitchen loomed with the usual dark monotony. No fairy Godmother had changed the house while I was out, sprinkling gold dust to illuminate the routine grey of the walls. No, it was all the same, invariable and unrelieved.

'You go and hang that bloody coat upstairs and be quick about it,' my mother shouted. 'You don't deserve to have anything decent, it won't last five minutes the way you go on — I wish Hannah could see you now, she'd be surprised. You deliberately defied me — I've a good mind to make you send it back to her. You'll wear that coat when I see fit young lady and not before.'

On and on I heard her voice from the step at the bottom of the stairs. I undid the buttons slowly, then stopped, seeing myself in the mirror. My face was tear-stained and blotchy, two puffy red eyes peeped out and my nose was red and running. I wiped it with the back of my hand. Straightening up I turned this way and that. The jacket was far too big — the shoulders stood voluminously over my own and the back hung in folds. The sleeves were creased from where I had pushed them back and it reached almost to my knees like a full length coat not a jacket. I would no doubt grow into it. Everything was bought too large so that you could 'grow into it'. You were always waiting it seemed, for that glorious golden time to come about when everything would be right and your clothes would fit. But you grew secretly and did not notice while things became shabby and worn. And you went constantly in old clothes with holes, for if anything was good you did not wear it until it matched the same worn greyness as the rest of your life.

I pushed my hands deep into the pockets and watched as something awful happened. In the reflection I could identify my face but there was nothing else of me. My head alone protruded, the survivor of a camel hair landslide, for there was fold upon fold of excess material. I knew as I hung it back in the wardrobe that it would never fit me. For in one short afternoon I had already outgrown the dream.

Florence and the Doctor

It was late at night when Aunt Nancy walked in breathless. 'Come quickly Nellie,' she said. 'Mother's had one of her turns again!'

That's what they used to call it when Great Aunt Florence became distant and stopped listening to those around her, when she stared past us for something else — one of her turns.

Her world was peopled with everyone that had ever lived and some that had not. It was so vast, teeming with life, that she became confused by it sometimes even calling these inhabitants by the wrong names, and feeling a bit put out by their irregular habits.

'Well he didn't give me any warning,' she would suddenly announce to the family, and turning to an empty chair would begin to scold. 'Fancy turning up like that without a word, and myself without a bit of bread to offer you.'

The family used to freeze with horror whenever it happened. If it was only to be a short conversation they would wait for it to end, politely without interrupting. It was when it lasted for days that they began to panic, imagining that they had lost her for good, or that she would never return to the ordinary sequence of events and to us.

'Florrie!' they used to call.

'Mother look at me!' said her eldest daughter.

'Run out and get some biscuits for our visitor,' was all Florence said.

Doctor Enbinder had been Florence's doctor for most of her married life. He had seen her safely through twelve pregnancies and it was a point of honour with him to always be at the graveside when any of the children were buried. I think he loved her as he would his mother, for he always made extra time for

61

Florence, and more importantly, he could talk her out of turns. Apart from him my mother was the only other person who had the ability to do this. Florence used to recognise them when she could not see anyone else for the dead that crowded in on her.

'When did it happen?' asked my mother struggling into her coat and picking up her shopping bag although everything was closed.

'This morning,' said Nancy. 'She's been like it all day. Dr Enbinder was with her this afternoon for an hour and he's been back with her since the close of surgery, but she doesn't see him. She keeps asking if the windows are blacked out and she's singing hymns all the while. She thought Dr Enbinder was a German soldier and he can't get through to her at all.'

It was a grey distraught man that greeted my mother's arrival.

'It's very bad Mrs McCrory,' he said. 'I can't break into her this time — it's up to you.' He passed the responsibility to my mother ungraciously, shaking with effort, exhaustion and emotion.

As Florence slept fitfully, they sat by her bed, but she only woke to see and curse Hitler who was stormtrooping the bedroom. Doctor Enbinder went home a shattered man and mother returned to us. Florence was sleeping through the blitz.

'Perhaps when she wakes it will be over,' said my father. But the next morning brought no change, despite an enterprising neighbour who dug out a union jack left from the coronation and urged Nancy to rush in waving it and announce V E Day.

'If nothing else dear, at least it will raise her spririts,' she said as she thrust it into her hand.

The entire street waited for the war to end that morning, but Florence was not fooled by propaganda.

'I read the papers,' she shouted to the advancing bread man who started to back away. By evening she had moved down to the cellar with a blanket and a hot water bottle.

Florence was drawing further and further away from us until she stopped seeing us at all. When she included us in what was happening to her it never seemed so bad, for then we were active participants in her personal history sharing the pain amongst us but when we ceased to exist for her and could do nothing — that was that what the family called a 'turn'.

We children were scared. We wanted our Florence back again. We cried around the kitchen table thinking that we had lost her for good this time. From the cellar 'Hail Holy Queen' was being sung in a thin treble.

'How long do you think she can stay down there?' said Leslie who was her youngest surviving son.

'Well that depends on whether mother had decided if it is the beginning or the end of the war,' said Rosetta, another daughter.

'Has anyone managed to find out?'

This calm acceptance of Florence's new life exasperated Leslie. He banged the table with the flat of his hand causing tea cups and family to jump.

'For God's sake!' he exclaimed. 'By your logic she could be down there for six years!'

After one night underground Doctor Enbinder could not take much more.

'She will have to go into hospital.'

Even as the family protested, they knew that he was right. He was a reasonable man.

'She can't be left alone for a minute. She needs constant attention. Look at yourselves!' He cast his eyes over the collection of relatives who had assembled in Florence's house since the previous day and were clustered around the table. 'You're nothing but shadows to her now.'

He was right. Being shadows it would make no difference to Florence whether she was with family or strangers. She no longer knew us and she had to be moved out of the damp cold atmosphere of the cellar.

'At least in hospital she will be kept in one place,' he added prophetically.

Matters this time played into the doctor's hands. Florence was easily convinced that he was an air raid warden and went happily into the ambulance.

'Don't cry,' she said, seeing us in tearful groups in the street. 'Being evacuated isn't that bad.'

The Great Northern Hospital was a Victorian institution that looked like a workhouse, situated on the Dock road, surrounded by railway yards, cranes and warehouses,. Florence was blissfully calm and, on entering the building and being surrounded by white coated workers, she thought that she was in a munitions factory and was going to do her bit for the war effort. She beamed and glowed with patriotism.

'Now get into the lift,' said Enbinder, the sweat beginning to stand out on his brow. He remembered Florence's past reluctant hospitalisations. But this time, in her fervour for Britain, she happily complied. The strain and concern of the last two days had worn the doctor down and, when the old iron lift stopped between the sixth and seventh floors, he pressed every button on the wall frantically before he discovered the alarm. He was acting like a man out of his senses he later admitted, for he left the alarm unrung, somehow fearing that this would upset Florence whom he was shouting at to stay calm and not walk around in the lift behind him. When he looked over his shoulder to see how she had taken it all, he saw her grinning from ear to ear and promptly fainted.

When the lift was retrieved from its limbo, the first thing the orderly saw as the doors opened was a man sprawled full length on the floor. Acting with admirable presence of mind he summoned a stretcher and Enbinder was sped off to casualty where it was discovered that he was suffering from stress and hypertension. No one apparently paid any attention to the white haired lady who, totally at peace with herself, was travelling up and down in the lift.

Later that evening Nancy was shocked when Florence walked in and went straight into her kitchen and calmly put the kettle on the stove.

'Those buses are dreadful,' she said looking round at the collection of relatives in her house with some surprise. 'I've been waiting ages for one.'

There was a stunned silence as Florence, obviously herself again, struck a match and lit the gas.

'You're all staying for tea I hope?' she smiled enthusiastically.

Touring Holiday

The confessional box swallowed me into its deep night's belly.

'Bless me Father for I have sinned.'

My voice reverberated off breathing walls that strained to hear. The sound loomed, hollow and amplified. A siren to guide lost ships through black, moonless water. A solitary star to chart the course by, sailing blind into the darkling. In the mist, shadows and drowned souls will try to pull it down. Hold on fast to the other side. Behind the grille, with grey head bent, the priest prompted crooking an ear in silent sea air.

My deep-mouthed sins hung lingering on sound, fading on the priest's ear, where they died as whispers.

'Father, I swore in anger, I was ungrateful and sinned against humility, and I told a lie.'

The disembodied voice of God's mouthpiece vibrated through the still air.

'To give way to anger is a failing, a weakness. We who are mortal, can only imagine the wrath of God for man's midsdeeds. Yet we allow ourselves to give in, and swear through our anger. I hope ye did not blaspheme?'

'No father, I did not.'

'Next time you feel moved to anger, offer up a prayer. God will never fail you. Now, what else? Oh aye — so you've missed mass — 'Tis a grave sin . . . '

'No father I haven't — I was ungrateful and told a lie . . . '

'Oh, yes! yes! You've been ungrateful. To your parents? To your teachers? . . . '

'Well, to the . . . '

'Ach, well, well,' the priest interrupted. ''Tis an awful thing not to show your gratitude — Our dear Lord offered up his life for us, and do we thank him? Do we get down on our knees every day and thank him? No! We do not. We go about our business, forgetting what he has done for us: everytime you show your gratitude, you are showing it to God as well. And you said that you lied — Oh, what evil is wrought by unsound tongues. You should never twist the truth, for in so doing you turn away from the light of God . . . now child you will say an act of contrition.'

'Father . . . humility,' I prompted, 'I have sinned against humility as well.'

'Oh, yes, yes . . . ' the voice hesitated. 'What did you . . . What way did you, er, er; commit this sin?'

'Father, I was proud.'

'Ah, 'tis a grave sin my child! The sin of pride is that same which Lucifer committed before he was cast from God's presence . . . You must resist the tauntings of that evil wretch and not be led into sin. But now my child, are you truly repentant? If you are, then ask, by the grace of God, for His forgiveness by making the act of contrition . . . '

The only sounds were vocal chords resounding like plucked strings left to quiver in my ear and the click click of rosary beads. My soul was beating against purgatory: Hear me!

'Through my fault, through my fault, through my own most grievous fault.'

Go in peace and sin no more,' the priest said.

I had been back for just a fortnight from a holiday in Ireland with my parents' neighbours. I was singled out by them because I was the nearest available child who was the same age as their daughter. I entered businesslike into the venture. She regarded me as an extra plaything; the touring holiday was mine if I was hers. A deal. We spat on the palms of our hands, spittle sisters.

My mother bought me new underwear to take with me. Five pairs of knickers with strong elastic, folded neatly into the case along with a new liberty bodice, three vests and the best of my old ones.

'If they ask you anything say you don't know,' she warned me, always frightened that one of us would let slip some ghastly truth about ourselves. 'They're only trying to find out things. Prying, pretending to be interested. Tell them nothing.'

That was her stock expression. 'Tell them nothing.' No one was to discover our skeletons carefully preserved with blanched bones. Aunt Mary was not married when she had my cousin, our Jack eats meat on Fridays, our cat shits under the sideboard. Pray for their souls.

'Don't let the cat out of the bag' she said, meaning the one room upstairs in which we all slept on account of the others being too damp. In our house, dark and uninviting rooms led off from brown painted corridors with bare bulbs weakly glinting. There was no carpet on the stairs and every time a door was opened, draught excluders made from old nylons had to be pushed back into place.

'You know what they say about the Irish don't you?' she laughed. 'That we let pigs run under the table while we are eating. Have you never heard that?' and she grinned, becoming more outrageous. 'They think that we wipe our forks on their backs! But listen now,' she added slowly, 'don't be making a holy show of me while you're away.' And with a look that belied her joke, she wagged a serious finger at me before I left, endowing me with awesome secrets.

At the wheel sat the girl's father, the sparse ginger strands of his hair which were combed over to conceal his balding head, shone like gold as they caught the sun. He had the pale and freckled skin of what could easily have been my ancestors, while I had the darker skin of others. He turned light colourless eyes full of pity as he offered me the world through hired car windows.

'You will never have the chance again,' he said with a finality that shocked me. He had an infallible view of the future. If the world was anyone's oyster, mine was to contain only grains of sand, irritants that had not come to fruition; while inside his daughter's he would make sure there were only the whitest pearls if it meant draining the sea to make it yield up its riches.

His wife sank back into the mock leather upholstery feeling the sweat stick the thin stuff of her dress to the seat. She crossed her hands in her lap and smiled a smug self righteous smile, queen of all she surveyed.

'Won't that rent-a-car sticker come off the back window Harry?' she asked peevishly.

We moved in quarantine, steadily advancing in our unburst

bubble which grew hot and smelt of nicotine and leathery polish.

'Close that window my hair's blowing out of shape,' she snapped at her daughter who sullenly began to sort out all the soft centres from a bag of sweets before thrusting the remains at me. She settled down reading a comic, sucking urgently as the Four Marys chased an interloper away from the hockey pitch.

Outside the car windows were sunsets and salmon-leap pink skies flecked with sea foam as the waves tore fiercely from the rough edge of the world. At Achill Island the land dropped abruptly and there was no more; only a faint rumour that the Isle of Saints and the Land Under The Waves were somewhere close-by.

'Bloody good job I've got strong brakes! Did you see the way that road dipped — and no warning! Bet there's many a drunken Irishmen ends up driving into the sea!' and they laughed, loud and long, enjoying the idea.

Out there, there was a dark lost world — in ancient times, miscreants were condemned to be cast adrift on it. They were given to providence with neither oar nor rudder, their ankles fettered and the keys thrown into the waves. Those same waves lapped at the coast with the gentle sleepy lovemaking of spray and rock kissing. Washed up along the beaches were the rusted keys returning as the upturned hide boats floated out of vision. Was that really just smooth white washed driftwood on the sand or was it the bones of Saint Patrick's persecutor picked clean by sea birds?

'You couldn't sunbathe on this beach, could you Harry' said the wife.

'I doubt if you could sunbathe anywhere in Ireland,' he said mockingly.

'It's too pebbly,' the daughter complained. 'And there aren't any beach huts, or cafes, not like when we went to Spain last year. I suppose that's why it's empty, everyone has gone somewhere better.'

Inland we drove around hill forts, mounds, tunnels and dolmens. Inside the passage grave, the stone walls were cut into patterns that spiralled, pulling me down until I could hear the sound of flint chipping, the echo of stone age carvers. I traced the walls with my fingers, feeling the impression of centuries.

'I'm cold, the daughter said. 'I can't see properly in this light — we might get sealed in.'

'Oh, we're going soon,' her father snapped.

'I'm not going on my hands and knees to get into that chamber Harry — I'm full of muck as it is. Don't they every sweep these places out?'

Back into the car, we drove past waterfalls that roared deafeningly of cattle raids, bulls' blood running over the grass and the screech of battlecry from a seagull born inland. Past tributaries and rivers up which the fair strangers came, manouvering in their skinny boats to conquer and loot and raze to the ground. The streams raced, carrying news and dead broken twigs, and the leaves scattered. Yellow gorse bushes burnt with black smoke air and I smelt a siege, the foul stench of Hell.

'Why are they burning the field dad?' The girl's eyes were large, and frightened.

'To keep the gorse down. Save having to chop it all . . . that would be too much work for them,' he mocked, implying that it would not be too much for him, a pale city dweller sitting behind a desk — not too much for him.

Untonsured monks drew up the ladder of the round tower sealing the door against the envoy from Canterbury, work of the devil.

There was a threat from that smoke, making us shudder. We drove past tinkers, dark strangers who stared at us. Their children ran barefoot after the car shouting. A swarthy man, bare to the waist was washing in a metal basin while a woman argued fiercely with him, a woman who pointed a knife she was using to peel vegetables and made stabbing motions in the air as if she would damage the vulnerable skin of his glistening back. His voice rose in anger and — bang! A hand was slapped down on the car by one of the children. A young girl with black hair everywhere held pink paper roses in one hand and with the other tried to force our windows down.

'Drive on for Christ's sake!' said the wife to her husband. And I was relieved, scared of these people who were not like us.

Draw up the ladder, seal the round tower. There were things to be frightened of, things to be in awe of.

The fairy rings that no one could stand inside for fear of being carried away, of taken inside a hill to the side where time ceased to exist. Like Bran I might be turned to ashes trying to re-enter the world. The worldly sun sloped behind the standing stones with their hypnotised circles. We followed the lay of the land as it curved, moulded, into the pattern of the cliff edge.

'Some good A roads would make all the difference,' he muttered and we rushed to enjoy the cold chintzed bedrooms of another one night bed and breakfast, with its congealing egg-and-bacon morning and cheap gilded mirrors.

Inside a single cell a tonsured monk, following orders, burnished gold over a thick white paste making the byzantine letters his own, weaving together the heads of small animals. A man tills the earth in a saffron shirt while, over his shoulder, an angel with finger pointing and the desire to understand drawn on his brows, looks on and asks — what is a lifetime? Is it the first letter completed? Circling the capital a dragon stalks breathing flames that scorch the text. Inside swim small colourful fish biting each others tails, threading through water.

I stood on a bridge holding a line, straining to see darting ripples where the stream reflected green and gold the quick silver fishes. Rainbows on the surface broke in arcs which grew faint. Here were plankton and thick weeds; green mossy slime sucking the float down.

'Have you got that float tangled? Pull the damn thing in!' he ordered and the line broke. Fishless, floatless, hookless I returned it.

'You've got to pay attention and not day-dream. Watch where you're casting out'.

He demonstrated, throwing his line expertly back over his shoulder to hurl it forward into the water where it dropped neatly. I tried to do the same. My line caught the trees behind and I was fishing leaves and branches until it broke for the second time.

'Well, that's you finished for the day, two bloody floats lost,' he said sweating, rather angry, his face becoming blotched with irritation. His daughter fished seriously in her father's image, delighted because I could not. I saw, in the shallow, bright pebbles, jewelled tiny shells and the shy movement of a small green crab. She did everything her father did even to exclaiming 'Women!' exasperatedly when her mother made the silly remark, bored, from the car. 'Women!' she said, nodding, smiling to her father (I'm the son you always wanted). 'Women!' (our private joke). She would not talk to me for the rest of that afternoon but walked ahead with her parents, linking them in a tight family bond. I was a failure with my pockets full of pebbles and shells; dry broken things.

Her husband's face had been yellow, butter leary, in the town.

'You can't get a decent cream cake in the whole of Cork,' said the wife.

Soda and brack and rich treacle farls, scone and fruit loaf, teased the salivary glands of my youth. Humpy-backed soda loaf, brown baked and floury topped, standing warm in the trays. Through the cracks the soft white pith showing. Thick black brack, shining with moist cherries, cut into slices on blue and white plates. Boozy cake stored in a tin to mature, drunk on porter soaking through slowly, inebriate Sunday five o'clock treat.

'Not a decent cream cake in the whole of Cork.'

That evening, outside the town, the woman of the house where we stayed tried to make me say *'go raibh maith agat'** as she cut soda bread.

'Go on,' she encouraged me, 'you've the tongue for it. Not like these Sassenachs, leave them to the Bearlagar.'

He simmered while his nose peeled, angrily, sun blistered. His eyebrows raised in irritation. His wife and daughter being left to the . . . what had she said, the mad woman? . . . while I tried 'Gurrammeeagit . . . gurameeagist . . . gurameejit . . . ohgurame-eagotyourself' until my courage drained away as the three travellers sat in stony silence. The wife looked haughty, head tilted back to observe the spectacle, disdain pinching her nostrils. The disapproval forced their daughter's mouth into a stiff line barely compressing her disgust.

'You're real Irish lookin',' the woman told me, smiling.

'Jewish lookin',' said her brother as he knocked mud off his boots outside the kitchen.

'Good lookin',' she said, passing him bread.

'What does it feel like to be told you look Jewish?' the daughter asked later as we prepared to sleep in our shared room.

'They crucified Jesus,' she added gleefully. 'They're often fat, and they have big noses and wear horn-rimmed glasses. That's what you're going to look like when you grow up — you're getting a double chin already you know. Look can't you just see it beginning to go loose under you jaw. I'd much rather be fair than dark,' she remarked as she began combing out her thin light hair.

I undid my heavy plaits.

'Isn't your hair straight,' she said. 'I always feel sorry for people

*'Thank you'

with straight hair. It costs them so much to have curls put in later. They should be able to have it done for nothing. My mum says I'm lucky because mine waves naturally. I think you look like that gypsy girl we saw earlier. Remember? The one with her hair all over her face. I thought she was a witch.'

A deal. I reminded myself that I had made a deal.

'I'm going to sleep,' I said.

Next morning the car seemed to move rather quickly along the dirt track letting the farm house shrink behind, its bed and break-fast sign creaking as it swung on unoiled hinges. He kept his eyes on the road, his face scornful.

'I'm finished with Ireland,' said the wife. 'Finished. I won't be back here in a hurry.'

God save Ireland. Finished with, the end of an affair. The pigs run under the table. They wipe their forks on their backs.

Suddenly the man looked up.

'Well,' he asked, as if he had a right, 'are you proud of your little drop of Irish blood?'

Lined and blotted on his brow were essays written in indignation by some crooked pen on a hot day. Scratch, scratch the nib wrote. British Constitutional History. The Empire. Little. Drop. His mouth sneered. 'Are you proud?' Why was there so much contempt for such a little drop? 'Proud of your little drop?' And drip, drip, I felt it drain away.

'But I'm English,' I answered, feeling like a foreigner.

Foreign blood. Is it green like a spaceman's or red like ours?

Drip, drip. Back into the mud from where it came. Drip, drip, on the pig's back.

'I'm proud to be English,' I said, feeling awkward and ashamed.

It was dusk. Dark blue shadows thrown by the powerful battery light flickered on the side of the tent as we hammered in pegs.

'These ridge tents are smashing things,' he enthused, delighted with his foresight. 'I knew it would come in handy to hire one. You never know where you might get stuck out.'

His wife supervised, walking from compartment to compartment, content in her own home.

'It's like an igloo!' she squealed happily, knowing she would not have to suffer any more mad women in the kitchen.

Outside the tent the knife I held slipped. Drip, drip, the little drop of blood.

'Can't you even peel a spud? And you think you're Irish! Mum, she can't peel spuds!'

They eat them skin and all, the dirt still on. Swallow mud and the pigs run under the table while they're eating. Squeaking. The way they talk. They don't wash. Pee in the field.

The sun fell into the edge of the field, spreading its blood-stained mark along the bruised sky. I could feel the earth tremble as I lay on the groundsheet, zipped with a circle into my own compartment. Through the floor I felt spiky grass, rough and flattened where I rubbed my hand. We were sealed inside by the fragile canvas membrane, soaked in its blue and orange womb-light as it rose and fell in time with us. I could feel myself sinking down, drawn by the earth's mangnetism until I reached the very core.

In the morning there were moisture spots on the steamy inner tent. Chilled air rushed in, stinging the wound, as he unzipped the fly sheet revealing the whole tent clammy, bathed in sweat. I smelt wet grass and my warm body evaporating heat. He left undisturbed the wife's compartment, where she slept on a camp bed avoiding contact with the earth and her husband. He was boiling up a pan of water on transparent blue methylated flames when she appeared — hair in curlers, feet in fluffy mules.

'Aren't there any showers?' was all she said, before grunting her way to the car. She began to make up her face, sitting in the front seat.

We were packing up when I saw two old men come along the road. I noticed them in the distance making their slow journey out to the fields. They approached, landscape camouflaged and grey earth clothed, drab capped and waistcoated, drawing close until I could make out their brown parchment faces and hands like roots. An elderly woman in a black shawl, and a younger swinging a basket, walked slowly to meet them. The younger planted her feet firmly, each step grew out of the ground.

'Damn!' cursed the wife as her green plastic heels stuck in the mud. The slow look of earth and sky meeting in inscrutable eyes saw her in red and green housecoat.

'Good morning,' said one of the men as they passed.

'We'll go into town and find some proper toilets with a plug point for shaving,' the husband said as we stowed the last vestige of our debris into the boot.

'I don't like the way they look at me,' she complained stroking her yellow hair, brittle to the touch. 'Those heated rollers are ruining it,' she muttered, checking that the purple eye shadow around her white eyes had not smudged.

Pink and orange synthetic sundress with smooth lilac plastic bangles and green muddy shoes. She clutched her fake straw plaited yellow handbag and adjusted her white rimmed sun glasses. Chic. In the baker's she queued with the sand and ochre people buying dun coloured loaves.

'Harry!' she shouted, deafening those around her. 'What shall I get?'

Out on the street he answered by shrugging through the shop window: how should I know?

'Shall I get some of these?' she enunciated, pointing, ignoring their glances as they turned wondering who she was talking to as much as at her accent. Their eyes were dazzled by the colours. Eyes that were used to a splash of rich crimson or cold sea green squinted at her, gaudy against the brown loaves.

On the day we were to leave, we saw warning signs. The sky clouded over and became dark and there was a sour wind. The ship bobbed up and down at its moorings.

'Oh God, that's all we need,' she uttered, taking fright at our whitening faces. 'Take one of these each and get into that cabin and lie down, the last thing I want is you two being up all night vomiting.'

The crossing was violent, the sea heaved and churned making our return painful so that the next morning, back on safe ground, we were left with a feeling of illness hanging over us. A nausea that dampened our spirits.

'Well, we're finished with Ireland,' she told my mother as she handed me over, smiling. 'I think we've seen everything there is to see — wouldn't you say so? I wouldn't want to go back for another holiday. I'd better be off. I must get some shopping . . . I just can't face doing it straight away though.'

'No, I didn't think you would,' said my mother, 'so I got you two pints of milk and there's some soda bread and tea and butter. At least you can have a cup of tea. Tell me, was it enough money we gave you for her keep?'

'Oh it was, no need to worry about that.'

'Well, thanks again for keeping her for so long. I'll bet you're exhausted. Would you like some eggs?' My mother touched my elbow to send me in to fetch them.

Everything was carried out on the doorstep. The two women rarely crossed each others thresholds. Once, when my mother was ill, she had come round carrying boiled fish on a plate for her, and my mother was embarrassed not knowing how to accept and hoping that she would not notice the damp patches in the bedroom. But she left quickly, would not even stay to drink a cup of tea, awkward about being over friendly.

'Oh God, you're a saint,' she told my mother, putting the eggs into her bag and clutching the wheel of bread under her arm. 'You know, I noticed one thing while we were over there.' She drew closer, becoming chatty. 'That for all they say about the Irish being great Catholics, I think it's far easier for them. Wouldn't you say so? They've become lax. They don't have to defend their faith the way we do.' She crossed herself piously, Catholic fervour glinting. 'And I feel the eyes burning me saying "Look at her, the brazen hussy" because I was showing my arms and wore no brazen hussy' because I was showing my arms and wore no stockings . . . Oh I don't forget the Irish girls that came here during the war. I saw Irish girls getting off the bus with men they'd only just sat next to. Oh yes, Irish girls were vulgar, some of them. Just because they were in England they thought they could do as they liked. Many's a one went back with a . . .' She lowered her voice, hesitating, looked around, then continued in a whisper, ' . . . a pig inside her — you know what I mean? And the likes of those were making sheep's-eyes at me because I didna't wear stockings.'

My mother nodded, trapped at the front door. She nodded, not daring to disagree.

Behind the wife on the pavement the daughter mouthed 'DO YOU GET ALL YOUR CLOTHES FROM JUMBLE SALES?'

'Any ideas what I can get for tea?' the woman continued. 'My two won't be satisfied with just bread and eggs. Honestly, if I didn't feed my family so well we'd be millionaires.'

Across my mother's face there was the trace of a laugh.

'My dad says we could buy our own car on all the money we spend on food,' said the daughter to no one in particular.

'Oh well, we're finished with Ireland,' the woman repeated, smiling at my mother.

'Why do the Irish all come to England if they're all so proud to be Irish?' Her daughter asked over-loudly. 'England must be better if they all end up over here, mustn't it mum?'

'They come over here to work,' said her mother.

'I thought no one worked in Ireland. Isn't that why the country's poor? Because they're all lazy and won't work? That's what dad said.'

'Of course not,' said her mother embarrassed, quickly turning to mine. 'Your husband is from Belfast isn't he?' To us children she explained, 'That's British. He's not really Irish you see. Of course it's different for you', and she smiled at my mother. 'A wife's place is with her husband. You have as much right to be here as . . . well . . . as me,' she finished doubtfully.

My mother's face had set awkwardly, the distance between them too great.

'It's time I got on with my work,' she said retreating into the gloom of our corridor.

I lingered in the street with the girl.

'I bet your great-grandparents kept pigs. Do they keep pigs in the North? I don't think I'll be playing with you in future,' and she skipped off.

'Did you ever keep pigs, Dad?'

'You know I bloody didn't.'

'Who's been putting those ideas into your head?' snapped my mother. 'Finished with Ireland, I ask you! Did you ever hear anything so daft!'

'I'm finished with you,' sang the daughter through our letter-box the next day, scared to come in. There might be pigs under our table spawning in mud. Avoid contamination. Shout through the door.

She took what she thought to be friendship and held it up to the light. Fragile, she saw that it would break easily. On my skin her trained eye saw blemishes that I had never noticed. And I became aware of the touch which was cold and impersonal. Revolted by it I shouted, 'Sod your bloody cream cakes and your touring holidays! Who said I ever wanted to play with you in the first place?'

'For shame. You're too proud. I'll tell mum what you said,' and the letter box slammed.

My postcard arrived a week after I was back.

'Having a wonderful time,' it said.

All Hallows

Throughout the day we were aware that something dangerous and frightening was about to happen. Tensions mounted and my mother came in looking pale.

'I've just seen a big heavy cockroach out in the yard, I couldn't bring myself to stand on it. There's a death on the way surely.'

The priests had already given out black edged slips of paper to the adults, who then wrote on them the names of the dead and sent them back sealed in envelopes. My father became mysterious every year at this time. Once, before I had learnt better, I tried to peer over his shoulder as he wrote. He covered the paper with his arm and looked around, panic-stricken. He dreaded being discovered, and he called for my mother to take me away.

'Don't ever disturb your father when he is filling out his mass card.' She too would busy herself in the kitchen until he had finished. None of us were to see the names of his past. My mother had to practise writing before she filled hers in. She would take down the jam jar of dried up biros and sort through them until she found the one that still worked. Laboriously she spelt out the names, moving her lips as she wrote each one three or four times. Her handwriting sloped different ways as she tried out which looked best. She went round and round the margin of the paper bag with its neat printed message:

MacCawley The Butcher of Quality: Pork, Offal, Home Made Black Pudding. Our Meat Always Fresh.

The names of her parents, her brothers, her sister, her half-sister, cousins, aunts, great-aunts and uncles, a school friend and the most recent of the neighbours. An endless list of names spun round in shaky blue clotted handwriting as the pen seized up and spluttered. The empty mass card stared from the fireplace; she only had one chance on that. When she was ready she would take it down, dreading making a mistake. She twitched the pen in the air over the paper, hesitating before bringing it down into contact. JOSEPH MORAN she started — the pen clotted on the last N of Moran.

It was the eve of November, the month of the dead. Although we knew that the assessment of souls in purgatory was not due until two days later when, on All Saints, we would pray for plenary indulgences, we knew that on the eve of November, as the sun set, hordes of spirits would try to reach the Kingdom of God without success. They began their upward journey impatiently, choosing not to wait and find out who amongst them has been granted remission. The majority of these were of the Lost — the legions of shades without hope who had been condemned to wander forever. On that night the mob would hammer against the closed gates pleading piteously for mercy and be shown none.

Evil roamed at the crossing of this month into the next. We could feel it. The angry dead revisited us, annoyed at being neglected all year. This was their time for rememberance and they presented themselves lively and real. Everyone grew thoughtful and particularly careful of what they said, in case their ancestors heard. Around this time my mother dreamt that members of her family presented themselves petitioning for help. Only one plenary indulgence per living person. Who would get it? Who would be on the receiving end? There was no way of telling, and it did not follow that it should be granted to the person the prayers were offered for.

'All this effort for God knows who,' my mother once said.

I made constant streams of 'Hail Marys' and 'Our Fathers' in my head, wanting to achieve some sort of a record; the endless repetition of sounds blocked out the fear of spirits lurking.

'I saw your Uncle Gerald last night,' she would say, and the threads of sound were offered up for Uncle Gerald. Or 'I saw our Arthur' and like weather cocks being blown in the wind we focused our intentions on Arthur, moving from one supplicant to another as directed.

Occasionally the dreams frightened my mother, but those that she worried about most were the ones that she could not understand. Like the big spider becoming engorged and swollen on the white-washed wall outside. It grew and grew until it became a gaping dark hole, its legs dissolving into cracks in the brick and she stepped through unable to stop herself. On the other side the house and yard shrunk behind her until they were nothing more than a black dot on the horizon which in turn grew into a black spider, larger and larger, until once again she was compelled to step through the dark hole it created. Backwards and forwards she was forced to go.

We paid much heed to mother's dreams, all of us attempting some interpretation. We listened in rapt silence while she recounted what she had seen.

'There was someone in our kitchen,' she began, 'last night. The house was quiet but I wasn't scared. I went out there and turned on the light. But I saw no one. Then I heard noises . . . sort of grunting it was, muffled . . . someone trying to talk as if they had a gag in their mouth. I looked around but I saw no one. Just as I was coming out something crashed down, a cup or a plate . . . I don't remember. I turned round sharp and there, on the floor, I could see its legs. Under the table, someone in a grey mac with a brown paper bag over their head. Lying on the floor, thrashing about. Every time I got near to pull the bag off, they rolled away from me. I knew it wanted to talk to me, but it was being stopped, and I was being stopped from helping it.'

Our eyes grew large in wonderment.

'Who do you think it could be?' she asked my father, terrified.

'Well, could you not recognise the mac?'

'But why were they being stopped from letting me see them?'

'Three dreams in a row,' my father said ominously. 'Three dreams in a row about the same person and you should have a mass said. It's one of the only ways the dead have of asking us for our help. Go and see Father Gormley,' he told her — not waiting for her to repeat the dream twice — 'describe it all to him and ask what he thinks. He can offer a mass for whoever it is.'

'Eternal light give unto them O Lord and let perpetual light shine upon them' we chanted.

Father Gormley tried to reassure us. 'The only people that can harm you are living, you need have no fear of those that aren't.' But I was weighed down with spectres. I prayed that my departed family had already entered Heaven.

The dead had no way of helping themselves, only our intervention had the power to alter things. One indulgence granted could make all the difference between life in light or life in darkness. The responsibility was enormous. Those who did not get through would have to wait a whole year to try again.

On All Hallows Eve mother went slowly round the house. She checked that the front door was firmly closed, then she went from room to room sealing up all the windows with rags. No one could slip in. The doors to all the rooms were kept shut, as if to stop a fire spreading. We all carried rosary beads around our necks tucked under our vests and mother took the small statue of Saint Anthony out of her handbag, where it was usually kept, and placed it in her apron pocket to keep it on her person. A tiny silver statue no bigger than an inch, it nestled in a small metallic container that covered the image of the saint like the shell on a snail. If we were confronted by a wandering phantom, she told us to make the sign of the cross. That and the rosary beads would protect us.

'They don't come to get us, for God's sake, Nell.' Father protested, at the preparations. 'Just remember to pray for them, sure that's all they're interested in.'

We lit candles.

'Oh well, it will put us in the mood for tonight,' he joked, wanting to disperse our fears.

'Candles flames will protect you,' mother had said as she bought up two dozen from the chandlers. 'I'll take these up and have Father Gormley bless them in time for Halloween.'

Every Sunday at the close of mass we each lit one. Mother said they would protect us throughout the week. We knew from somewhere that evil spirits were terrified of candles and would seldom venture indoors where there were some. We preferred candle flames. Electric light illuminated the dark corners where shadows lurked but it was not the correct sort of light. We needed the flickering kind that allowed spirits to hover, so that their existence, which was what we required, was not denied.

We played games and told stories to divert our attention. As the sun set we would gather around the fire for safety huddling together, telling television ghost stories to take our minds off the real dead who were clamouring at our elbows. The aunt who lived alone always stayed with us on that night and would not return to her own home until daylight had exorcised the spirits from her cold kitchen. Great Aunt Florence would choose that night, above all others, to be extra communicative to her lost ones. All Hallows was a very great strain on her as one child after another struggled to get her attention. She had so many people to see, despite keeping up a constant dialogue with her dead throughout the year. All Hallows was a time of extra effort. Her knuckles stood out in her coarse red hands. The blue veins were knotted across the backs as she stared straight ahead mouthing prayers silently.

'Ah, sure, I never wanted the money,' she suddenly said, shaking her head.

'What did you say?' mother asked. But Florrie did not hear, she was already lost in conversation.

'All right, all right now: I'll put it in me purse. Ach, you shouldn't have come all this way — I wasn't bothered about the debt at all. Now are you sure you can afford this? I don't want you leaving yourself short. How's Ernest? Still his back is it? Is he still on the sick? Now, look, look — you take this here back,' and she waved her empty hand away from her. My mother stopped pouring tea and watched.

'Didn't she look well?' Florrie said to her.

'Who?'

'Why, Mrs Humphries!' and she pointed to the door the visitor had just gone through.

'Oh, Aye'

'She's had her hair permed — it's gone a bit frizzy. She says the heat's wild.'

'What heat?'

'The heating in them new flats they've moved to — you can't turn it off. It just comes on like magic — there's white boxes all over the place, pumping out heat — that's what's made her hair dry up.' She patted her own, silver white under the hair net.

'Mine's natural,' she said with pride. 'Here, Nell — I don't want this. Fifteen bob and him on the sick! Give it to the kids.' Her hand held out air.

'No, no Florrie, you keep it — it's too much, and besides it was a debt,' said mother, pushing it away as she got on with pouring the tea.

Florrie went rigid, the transaction forgotten. Her eyes became bloodshot from concentration and her breathing came faster and faster. She began to rock back and forth hugging her shoulders.

'Florrie's off again,' mother said cocking her head in her direction, and my father shrugged.

'May as well leave her.' For wasn't this the one night we would have loved to be able to join her in the strange world she inhabited all year. We admired her ability to deal with the spirit world in such matter of fact terms.

She sat up with a jerk. Her eye was clear and visionary. She had recognised someone. Often a great smile of relief spread over her face, the journey had been successful.

'All I said was, that we'd be going heathen and eating meat on Fridays at those prices,' she said angrily, wagging a finger. 'I never said you gave short measure!'

Her relief soon passed into annoyance, as she continued an ancient argument with the fishmonger.

'Ach, you're too expensive by half, that's why I took my custom up the road to the new feller. Nice shop he has. Little fishes swimming in a glass tank, and everything laid out on ice — not buzzing with flies like yours. Well, I'm sorry if it has upset her, but you tell your wife, she'll understand. It's nothing personal — she's a housewife like meself. With all those children — seven, eight is it? How many? Oh, God — I've had twelve, thirteen maybe — all eating fish they were. Grown up now, some of them. Joey?'

Her eyes peered into the distance. 'Joey? Is it you? my little one — you'll not forget your old mother' and her hand patted the air around her, stroked her child's head, as she rocked him on her knees crooning. 'Joseph — Joseph — you're back — my little boy, my dear one. Niall!' she shrieked excitedly. 'Look at him sleeping!' and with one arm she scooped up the tiny baby. 'Ah, you'll no grow any bigger,' she said, the tears beginning to pour down her face. 'You'll always stay my baby.'

I imagined that I could see, one after the other, a procession of her pale children as they rose wraith-like from the ashes to hold their mother's hand and comfort her. Florrie sat quietly, with a beatific smile on her face and her eyes misty.

'Here — see if she'll drink a cup of tea,' said mother, passing a cup and saucer.

'Florrie! Florrie! are you all right? Here's a cup of tea — will you take some tea?' Father repeated it seeing he was getting little response.

'Who are you?' she said looking at him strangely. 'Where are you from? She took the tea he offered and sipped it slowly, trying to remember if she knew him from somewhere.

'Tell me,' she said, trying to work out by elimination who he was. 'Did I put your name down on me mass card?'

That night we even took nightlights to our beds, so no spirits would disturb our sleep. Outside the night sky was thick and teeming as the rejected swarmed into it. The wind carried their voices, panes of glass rattled in every window. The underworld was massing.

From sepulchres and shallow graves they came: from unmarked unknown places. Crawling from under flagstones, bent double from tunnel graves. They flocked from cairns, barrows, and pits. They came from chapels and vaults. From family graves with well incised tombstones, their history laid out chronologically. Who was the daughter of the son, of the first to be buried, their names becoming obscured by the soft mossy growth. Suicides lay in unsanctified ground, away from the light. Their act of self-destruction, the gravest sin, denied them rightful burial. I thought about them, those friendless spirits, that no one could help to push upwards, for whom no prayers counted. They were the real outcasts. Forgotten, even in death.

That night everything was on the move; the clouds drifted and even the stillness of my room was disturbed. The wallpaper shifted as I stared, re-arranging the floral pattern into ethereal wreaths. Semi-human faces peeped out from behind foliage, half animal, wild spirits. I closed my eyes quickly to shut out the dead, but that night my dreams were heavy with black crêped mourners and the all pervading smell of damp and rotting leaves.

All Saints day dawned calmly with a still November sky. We celebrated those in Heaven and felt as if a great burden had been taken from us. It was with a sense of relief that we prayed for those still in purgatory the following day, for we no longer carried on our shoulders the weight of the entire other world.

It would be a year before we had anything to fear from wayward spirits. A year before those feelings buried deep within us would stir again, remnants from our dark and savage past. Feelings which the Catholic Church could not sanctify or explain away.

Linguistics

Sometimes Mrs Riley had the feeling of being left out in the cold by her family, now that the children had all grown up and left home. Of course she got a card every Christmas from her eldest son and his wife out in Australia, and her two daughters always came home for that particular holiday, but that still left her with 51 weeks to get through.

She blamed unemployment; it had forced her children away in search of work, and she blamed education; it had driven them away from home. Of the two she thought that eduction was the chief cause, because even if the factories had not all closed down, even if there were jobs locally, her children would still have moved in search of the new, hoping to find something better. As if they dreaded growing into what she had become.

Whenever she tried to explain how she felt her husband always said that she ought to see a doctor and it annoyed her to hear him talking about how women always went a 'bit peculiar' when they got to her age. He always stressed the fact that she was getting older while ignoring that he was too, for he was six years her senior. Once she tried to remind him but he just dismissed her saying that it wasn't at all the same for men. Even before Mrs Riley had reached the age that he was criticising she had found it difficult to explain anything to him. He seldom listened and when he did he never understood. After a few years she hardly tried anymore and on the rare occasions that she did, it only served to reinforce her opinion that it was just not worth the bother.

Their life together had gradually decayed until they hardly spoke to each other. At home there was a residual quiet, an organic silence that had grown over years until it bound their lives together. It was not a silence of thoughtful contemplation but a silence from a paucity of words. There were not enough to go around for Mr and Mrs Riley. Their world was a series of silences joined only by expressions for basic needs. Food, warmth, sleep, sex. A blow, a kiss, a smile, expressed their emotions and gradually became them, the full extent that was left.

She would sit facing him and feel water rushing past her ears. Insults went so deeply into her that they would not surface. She could not recall them. She could not say what it was that had hurt her while she felt the pain keenly. She wanted to say: 'Today I felt all my inside just go away and I was empty, a receptacle ready to receive the world pouring in through my eyes. I wanted to drink it up, because I had lost all the old stale things and in their place I wanted to pour sunlight clear and warm. If I could drink it I would become golden and glowing. And I knew that today would be the day on which I would learn to float, if I was ever going to. Out over the courtyard, the factory, the iron swings, out into the light. I felt breathless all day, thinking that I could say anything.'

Instead what came out was: 'I felt dizzy.'

'Hrummph.'

'But I don't anymore.'

'Hrmmph?'

Her husband was a man of few words, who used even less when his wife was around. He had no interests, or none that he would talk to her about. She needed something. His company was not enough.

'Join an evening class' the poster said and she scanned the list for something that she might be able to learn.

There was not a lot on offer at the local centre. She did not fancy the cookery or dressmaking and that did not leave her a lot to choose from. There was something called 'the art of make-up' but as she had reached this stage without mastering *that* she did not think that it would make a lot of difference if she was to give it a try now.

Her finger went down the list. Car mechanics. But she did not have a car. Woodworking, mathematics . . . she knew that she could not do either of those. Art? Well it would be useless her joining that course. Art was all portraits and stuff, horses' heads and vases of flowers. She could not even manage to hold a pencil still long enough to draw a line without getting bumps in it. The ability to draw was one of life's mysteries. It was a wonderful gift that never filtered out to her reaches. She was impressed by anything that looked right — a head in the correct place, feet pointing the same direction. Statues she found a bit harder. There was a man outside the town hall, over-large and turning green, he stood there in all weathers. And she had seen odd cast iron shapes placed in parks by the council. She thought that they were made in shipyards and like the housing plans had little to do with her. But pictures you could hang up on walls. One of her neighbours had a print of three white horses charging into the sea over the mantel-piece. Their manes were thrown back in frenzy as they urged themselves on to destruction. It seemed funny to Mrs Riley to be cooking the tea in the kitchen under the sight of the horses in the next room. No, art was a pretty daft thing for her to do.

French? Her finger stopped. One thing that she had always wanted to do was to travel. She would love to go to France, but he did not see the point. He called them 'Frogs' and said that they smelt and he did not like them. He had never met any, but that did not stop him disliking them. He did not like many people really. She found herself wondering who or what he did like.

'What would we do when we got there?' he had said on the one occasion that she had been stupid enough to suggest them both going.

'I don't know what we'd do,' she had answered, forced to feel as if she had said something unbelievably stupid. She did not know exactly what to expect or what to promise it would be like.

'I just thought that it might make a change instead of going up to your brother's again,' but her voice had no conviction under his disbelieving gaze. She faltered. What had she been thinking of?

'Where do you think we'd stay? What would we eat? Not that foreign muck I can tell you. Oh no, no indeed! They're not clean, don't wash their hands after they've been to the toilet. It's very different out there, not a bit like home.'

She had never mentioned it again. Her children had been all over the place. She envied them when the postcards started arriving during the summer. Her daughter went to Switzerland once and sent back a card showing snow capped mountains and fir trees. Mrs Riley thought that it must have been cold there, but when Caithlin came backs she was suntanned.

'How did you manage that?' she asked her incredulously.

'Oh mam, it's not all blizzards and snowstorms you know. It gets quite hot too. How do you think people ski? They can't do it in bad weather.'

Mrs Riley had been stunned. Sun and snow together? It didn't seem right.

'What language do they speak then?' she asked. But her daughter would not be serious and told her that they spoke French, Italian, or German depending on which area they were in.

'Don't be soft! You mean to tell me that I could be on a bus talking French and it would go into a street and we'd all speak German! You must think that I was born yesterday,' and her daughter had laughed.

She turned away from the poster. It was partly her own fault, this boredom, she was sure of it. When her daughters were there at least she had someone to talk to. It was being there with him all the time that got her down. She didn't mind being on her own either, but it was in the evenings when he would just sit there without saying a word that she felt uneasy. She remembered when the youngest girl had been studying . . . oh, what was it called?. . . anyway, she had brought home this funny book all about restricted codes and figures of speech. She had tried to have a quick read of it on the sly, and got stuck on a bit about parts of the brain never developing due to the narrowness of the mental images caused by the repeated use of confined expressions. And there was an entire section that she couldn't read through about working-class children in the education system being at a disadvantage before they had even started because of the restrictions on the speech patterns, or something.

Mrs Riley imagined that it worked like a cinema screen in the head. Some of the screens weren't in cinemascope and so a lot of details were missed out, projecting onto the curtains and blurred around the edges. She felt awful. She had stopped her child's brain developing! She and her husband must have been prime examples. And she felt really upset to think that the only language she spoke was restricted.

She would have liked, then, a language of her own to say secret things in. Something personal that she need have no fear of. She thought once of learning morse code so that when he grunted she could reply in 'dot-dot-dot-dash-dot-dash-dash-dash.' That might make him listen.

Then one day it came to her. She was struggling with a knitting pattern. She had gone wrong and was going to have to unpick the last few rows and she re-read what she should have done. The symbols that they used always fascinated her, and the abbreviations always looked so odd. Neither of her daughters could knit. Cathlin said that she just could never follow the pattern and the other never had any patience with practical matters. Mrs Riley loved solving a knitting pattern. She felt that she was taking up a long list of letters and meaningless numbers and translating them into a solid thing, in this case a jumper.

Then she had a wonderful idea. It was so simple she wondered why she had not thought of it years ago.

KNIT TWO PURL TWO SLIP STITCH PASS SLIP STITCH OVER NEEDLE WOOL AROUND NEEDLE TWICE KNIT TWO TOGETHER. K2 P2 PSSO YRN A N K2 TOG MAKE LOOP WIND YARN AROUND FINGER

She would knit everything that she wanted to say! She would knit her life into a knitting pattern. It would be her own private language.

She took up knitting seriously. She was unable to stop once she got started. Someone could have set fire to the house and she would not have noticed.

'Is tea ready?' he asked one night while she was engrossed. He had to ask again. He was hungry and beginning to feel irritable. 'I asked you if the tea was ready,' he repeated louder this time.

Although her lips were moving he had to strain to hear, it sounded like meaningless numbers to him.

'What did you say?' he asked, beginning to feel worried.

'K2 tog. sl st o, yrn rn n, K1., K4, P2, to end.'

'?'

'K2 tog,' she said loudly and smiled.

Mrs Riley soon discovered that she could tell her knitting everything, so she made sure that she took it with her wherever she went. Before she left the house she would check that she had enough balls of wool to be getting along with. It made everything seem so much more tolerable. Before she took up knitting she had always hated doing the laundry. But encouraged by the wool in front of her she began to play more. She tried experimenting with different soap powders, to vary the routine a bit by mixing them in the machine to see the different effects. She started to knit up the tale of her experiments.

It was on one particular day, when she was knitting the story of the mixture of a new blue biological sort and a gentle grey-looking powder that was not supposed to foam, that she was disturbed by a neighbour.

'That's clever. What pattern are you using?' asked Mrs Ideal Homes who lived a few doors down.

'Oh, none really, Mrs Homes, I sort of make it up as I go along.'

Mrs Riley thought of how she had been knitting the tale of the white shirt she could see spinning behind the glass front in the machine. It was pale and sodden on account of its life of drunken debauchery. Its beer stains had clearly marked it out as a sinner to the cleansing power of the Blue Flash which would overcome the toughest grime, convert it back to the rightful path. She made three white bobbles by knitting the wool around the needle and going back into the stitch until each bobble stood out from the background on a raised surface. She looked at them with satisfaction knowing that they were the buttons in the tale.

'What is it then, a pullover?'

'I don't know, I'll have to wait and see.'

Mrs Ideal Homes looked blank.

'Pardon?' she asked, thinking that she must have misheard the answer, 'I don't think I've understood . . . '

'Well it's nothing,' said Mrs Riley , holding her knitting away from her and inspecting it. It was a white and green shape with textures from where she had changed the stitch. 'I suppose you could wear it around your neck,' she suggested lamely to her neighbour. 'But it doesn't make that much difference, I'm just doing it. I enjoy it.'

Mrs Ideal Homes glared at her as if she had been deeply insulted.

'I don't understand that, I really don't,' she muttered more to herself than to Mrs Riley. 'I'd never do that' and she shook her head and went to unload the spin dryer. 'Just look at all the wool you're using up. That's a waste that is.'

She sounded as if she had been slapped in the face, she was both petulant and angry. Mrs Riley carried on with her knitting, a look of indescribable calm on her face. She was knitting a message to Mrs Ideal Homes right then. It said: Leave me alone to do what I do, while I will leave you alone to do yours.

As soon as she had finished the row a feeling of relief broke and she forgot about the other woman who was emptying the machine. Her own washing was going through its second stage, becoming whirling kinetic sculpture. Flashing colour behind the glass. The second compartment of washing powder was being used and it started to froth up, white and mountainous, reminding her of the postcard. White-covered fields, sheets and vests, unspoiled. Like Switzerland. Snow in England turned to slush, grey-black and slippery. Or froze. Old people fell and broke their hips. The streets did not all get gritted, so some people became trapped indoors. Heating bills were horrendous. Winter in England was sitting in the kitchen with the oven on, scared to use the central heating which heated all the hall and then he would have to pay for it.

'Bloody ridiculous this,' he'd say. 'Hot enough to grow tomatoes on the landing. When they put in these things did they think that anyone was going to sit out on the stairs all night?'

The council would not put individual controls on the radiators, so he had bought a second-hand electric fire with three bars to it and they did not switch on the heating at all.

The mountains of Switzerland were being turned around and around rinsed with water. Her face reflected to her like the victim of a ship-wreck in the glass portal. Behind it she could see the effect as continents were wiped out. Mountains toppled into the sea. So much destruction.

She sang as towns were destroyed, she screamed and people fell dead, stricken. Trains stopped running, cars collided on the motor-ways. She saw it all in a flash. Forcing herself, she laughed, and the sea swelled its belly, swallowing the coast. She could hear rumbling in the distance, of rubble, bricks, and whole continents collapsing. Twenty thousand years of wind and soil erosion were being compressed into two minutes. Volcanoes erupted, lava encased her. She was going to be preserved as a statue and kept in a glass case in a museum.

'What are you cooking for tea?'

Mrs Riley crashed back into reality, drawn into the life of the launderette once more.

'I don't know,' she answered vaguely.

She had stopped cooking weeks ago. She discovered that she could just as easily buy a ready-made steak and kidney pudding, or open a tin of beans. George would eat whatever was put in front of him.

'*I'm* making a chilli I found the recipe for in my woman's magazine,' Mrs Ideal Homes continued, looking greedy. 'Did you see this week's? There are some lovely recipes in it for eggs and pasta — you know, what they eat in Spain. I've bought some garlic. Have you ever tasted garlic?'

Nancy looked up and grinned weakly.

Her neighbour continued excitedly, without wanting a comment 'Oh, I'm a real devil' drawing out the word de — vil to emphasise it. 'I don't like to be ordinary,' she giggled, putting her hand across her mouth discreetly in case her teeth fell out.

'Well, you've got to use your imagination haven't you? That's what I say — may as well not be boring. Bert says I'm a . . . something . . . woman.'

She thought hard of what it was that he had said, and couldn't remember the word he had used.

'Oh, you . . . something . . . woman,' she repeated, 'because he never knows what he'll get for his tea.'

Her voice was high and squeaky with girlish glee at the half-remembered compliment: 'UN PRO-DICK-TABLE,' she repeated slowly, as the meaningless word came back to her in phonetics.

Then her voice dropped and her eyes widened. She was going to tell Nancy a truth, a secret pearl of wisdom.

'I feel sorry for some men, you know,' and she looked at Nancy for the first time since she had re-opened their conversation.

'Their wives can't be bothered. It's laziness, that's all, and lack of imagination, we can't all have that,' she added smugly. 'But you know what they always say — The man's heart and the way to find it. I mean . . . ' and her voice slowed down as she came to the crucial part of her message. 'It's one way of making sure that they keep coming home.'

Nancy had caught only the last two words and, fearing she had been asked a question, pretended to show interest, in the hope that it would be repeated.

'Coming home?' she said. 'Who?'

Mrs Homes gave her a pitying look. She could obviously see into the future and had read the score already.

'Why your husband dear!'

Nancy did not like the way she said that. It sounded like 'you fool'.

'Well I can't stand here talking all day,' Mrs Homes said irritably. 'Some of us are busy, some of us take a pride in our homes.'

Nancy's lack of concern put the other in a tantrum. The calmer one was, the hotter the other became. Cramming socks into a black polythene bag she strode out clutching her sack in front over her stomach like a phantom pregnancy.

Nancy, left at peace, had started to knit two lamb chops be-having conventionally. Holding hands.

Kings

'I shall bless the house in which the image of my heart is exposed and honoured.'

That is the promise Jesus Christ made as his heart bled in anguish. Did he know that after this all Catholic families would have a picture in which he would be shown opening his tunic, to reveal a valentine's-type heart surrounded with a crown of thorns which cruelly dug in? Had he known what it would look like, would he, I often wondered, have made such a rash promise? Surely there must have been a less gory way to illustrate that salvation would only come through pain?

The message was carried down for generations. For salvation there must be suffering. Another thorn, another nail.

I hated the picture. The face of Jesus Christ was too sorrowful. I caught my breath and felt pains in my chest whenever I looked at it. Our next door neighbours found the image so repulsive that they nailed it to the inside door of a wall cupboard. When the priest came round the door was left open. As soon as the visit ended the door was shut, the picture banished to darkness.

My parents of course, insisted on giving it pride of place. The first thing to hit anyone between the eyes as they entered the living room was the sweet heart of Jesus dripping blood. I found it more frightening than any horror film, more real than reality, for I had learned that this was an absolute truth. No stage-trick this, no fake red pellets but the Son of God exuding human blood. A constant reminder that he had suffered for us and we should suffer in turn for our eventual glory. It was passive submission, to accept the crown of thorns, the scourging, the death agony, for redemption.

An air of righteousness constantly hung about us. He was the

Son of God, we knew. The fools and philistines had killed him. We alone held the truth and were carried along hopefully because the weak would one day inherit the earth.

One day my mother came home carrying something under her arm wrapped in brown paper. It was a tea tray. Metal, cheap, crudely made, showing a man with long flowing locks on a white charger crossing what appeared to be a stream. An old woman in her 90s, that my mother occasionally did shopping for, had forced it on her by way of a present.

'Silly old fool; she found out that you were from Belfast, now there'll be no stopping her,' she said to my father as if it was all his fault for coming from the wrong province.

'I often suspected that she'd been "Lodge" in her day. I didn't know what to say. Thought it might distress her if I said I was a Catholic, so I just asked her for something to wrap the bloody thing up in.'

She held it away from her and looked at it, beginning to laugh.

'Oh God, just look at the thing! Isn't it a sight? The long hair on him, all in ringlets, it's down to his waist! She said it would look smashin' over the fanlight — can you see that over the door and Father Gormley not able to set a foot inside? That would be a great joke that would. Me up at confession on Saturday "bless me father, but I've been idol worshipping" Sod that! What'll I do with it?' she asked and crashed it down on the table.

'Who is he?' I asked.

'Ach, he's a right old bugger, that's who he is.'

Bloody King Billy, as I eventually discovered his name to be, was the Protestant version of our Christ the King. Only, unlike ours, he was an earthy king. A temporal monarch who fought in battles. Proud, triumphant, the antithesis of the sorrowing spiritual king, who with passive gesture pointed mutely to his suffering. Billy carried a sword with which to take life, while our king sacrificed his own life, volunteering to have it taken.

She put it behind the sideboard, face to the wall so we wouldn't have to look at it. But it annoyed her: she knew it was there. At night she would sit in the room feeling irritated, repeatedly glancing towards the far wall. She began to itch.

'I swear I've caught a rash since that sod's been in the house!'

It gave her no rest, lurking behind the sideboard, ever watchful.

'I can't eat me dinner in peace.'

She began losing weight. By the end of the week she had had

enough. On Friday she announced that she was putting it out for the binmen.

'Oh God, Nell, you can't put it out by the bin!' my father said looking horror-struck. 'One of the men on the wagon's certain to be Orange Lodge.'

In my father's eyes already were the pale flickerings of fires as our house burnt down around us. The clear grey of his irises were shattered, as bricks were hurled through the windows. The siege mentality held him in its grip.

'Oh, for God's sake! I won't leave it by the bin then. I'll just go out when they come and ask them if anyone wants it.'

'What! Be seen in the street with a picture of King Billy!'

His eyes were wild this time, fearing reprisals. The secret societies of agrarian Ulster that had flourished in the 19th century were apparently still prepared to lynch my father. Defenders and Peep 'o' Day Boys who would drag him from his bed at dawn still lurked somewhere in Toxteth. The past lived on in the present, not allowing a solution. It seemed as if we were struck with the offending object.

My mother looked desperately around, the way the mouse had last winter before the cat caught it with its paw for its final and fatal mauling. Suddenly her face relaxed into a smile. Her eyes were fixed on the coal bucket that had been left by the fire, forgotten about in all the excitement. Everything it touched became soiled and grimy. Coal dust always spilled out onto the carpet. Father followed her gaze.

'I'll take that back out to the coal hole,' he began.

'Here!' Mother called him back. 'Here's a lid for that bucket, it will stop the dust flying around.'

I will never forget the scratched and sooty face of the King, a prisoner in our coalshed; nor the triumphant rattle and scratch of coals as my mother raked them in with the gusto each time.

'I'll fetch the coal,' she would say, springing to her feet lightly to volunteer for the job we all hated.

She became eager to blacken her hands and wore the stigmata of grime proudly as the dust trapped itself in her bitten-down cuticles, weathering into her coarse calloused palms. We would hear her grunting with effort.

'You Bastard!' she cursed out in the dark as she scraped and ground the shovel unnecessarily on the tray. She would finish by slamming it down in fury with a resounding clang to hail the completion of her task.

When she came back into the kitchen she always had a high colour in her cheeks, which was more than the flush of physical exertion. It spread onto her face from an inner glow, a sense of tranquility and well-being that shone in her eyes. And I always thought that she was at her most peaceful when calmly stoking up the fire under the loving gaze of the Sacred Heart.

Tell Her Finny Says Hello

Years later Ronnie Morgan could never quite describe how it happened. The man just stepped up in front of them and neither she nor her brother noticed where he came from or whether he had been following. But the man stood in their way and then changed his mind for he was apologetic, trying to step out of the way sideways so that they might continue. He did not want to force them to a standstill. That was not his style. But he wanted them to stop of their own accord. He willed that they might just stop for a few seconds so that he could address them. Yet when they did he hesitated as if he could not decide. When he finally spoke to them he was extremely polite, even cautious.

'Excuse me' he began, which was odd to them because adults did not usually ask children to excuse them, 'but did I just hear you call her Ronnie and she called you Frank?'

The sound of his voice surprised them. It was different, soft and drawling not quite American. The two children froze. They stared at him wondering who he was and what he meant by his question. Neither answered. The man recognised their distress and, of all things, blushed. Again this was not a reaction either child expected from an adult. The man rushed on with his explanation to ease his own discomfort as much as the children's.

'It's just that . . . I'm terribly sorry to intrude like this but would it be . . . could it be that your surname's Morgan?'

This time it was Ronnie that he spoke directly to. He had judged correctly that by the way the boy was holding on to her hand she was likely to do most of the talking, or take charge.

'Well yes it is,' she said bewildered by the question.

'Veronica and Francis Morgan?' the man asked. Seeing them nod, his face broke into a broad grin. 'Veronica and Francis

Morgan!' he exclaimed as if he still could not believe it. 'Well I never, I'll be darned!' and he threw his head back with a yelping noise.

Frank noticed that he had two gold fillings and otherwise perfect teeth. He was dressed in a low zoot suit made out of a checked material. The jacket was cut very tight and long over the hips with broad and obviously padded shoulders. He wore a black felt trilby with a woven band around the rim. They had never seen anyone before who looked like him. Ronnie noticed the flecks of yellow and blue in the grey suit which from a distance melted into a darker check. It looked soft and comfortable. She would have liked to run her hand over it because it looked as though it would be pleasant to the touch. It was definitely the nicest material she had ever seen.

'And your mother? Her name's Elisabeth — Right?'

'How did you know that?' Ronnie asked and glanced at her brother in surprise.

The man smiled seeing that they were intrigued. He unbuttoned his jacket and put his hands in his trouser pockets. The jacket fell in soft folds behind the crook of his elbows.

'I'm an old friend of your family's. Why I knew your mother when she was no bigger than you are now.'

This was irresistible to the children. Their faces relaxed and changed as they became curious. Frank forgot his reserve. 'Really! you knew her when she was the same age as me?' he asked excitedly.

'Sure did, we used to play out on the street together.'

Ronnie and Frank couldn't imagine their mother bouncing a ball or skipping, lively and playful.

'What was she like?' demanded Frank.

'Oh she was real pretty' the man said smiling slowly and nodding his head, pleased with the memory their mother had left in him. Oh yeah . . . real pretty; just like your sister.'

He said it so straightforwardly. To him it was merely stating a fact. He looked at her and smiled. Ronnie felt her face get hot and she looked at the pavement. No one had ever called her that before. She put the toe of her shoe into the crack between the flat stones and moved her foot about pretending to be intent on some game and not to care about what he'd said, although her face was flushed with pride. Frank asked question after question unabashed and Ronnie listened while the man tried to remember everything he could about their mother when she was a girl.

'I can't imagine her with long black hair. It's short now and it's grey mostly,' Frank told him.

'Ah but when she was a girl it was thick and shiny and she kept it tied back in a single heavy plait. Always with a bright ribbon tied in a bow at the end, like your sister's now.'

Ronnie looked up. 'You have your mother's eyes too,' he said looking squarely at her.

'Everyone says that Ronnie's like mam.'

'She certainly is,' the man agreed. His gaze was so insistent *that* was what Ronnie remembered years later — the way he looked at them, with hungry eyes. Like a blind man who, recovering his sight, wants to see every small detail and never becomes tired of just seeing, content to look without comment, so the man wanted to look at them.

'When I see you I feel as if I'm looking at Elisabeth, only she's ten years old and I'm still in short pants.'

Ronnie started to laugh and the man, relieved to hear her, joined in. The girl was aware that it was not her but her mother that he looked at, while in Frank, she wasn't sure. He seemed to see someone else besides the small boy. It was as if he recognised another person with whom he was familiar. But he was entirely a stranger to them as he stood with his hands in his pockets. His wrists were narrow, fine boned with a powdering of dark hairs. Ronnie was fascinated and delighted by the notion of such a smart man being an old friend of their mother's, their mother who was now so dull and worn but had once been bright and eager — a child, a young woman. She decided that he must have been an admirer.

She could not remember how long they stood talking but it was long enough for her to stop feeling awkward with him and although she let Frank do most of the prompting for more stories about their mother, she stopped pretending to be only half listening and did not disguise her curiosity. She tried to look hard and long at him but he would always catch her eye and start grinning, and she felt that it was impolite to stare for too long.

The lasting impression she took with her was the absolute difference between this man and anybody else that she had ever seen. But she could never describe what it was; it was much more than appearance. Of course he looked different. Neither she nor her brother had seen men dressed in anything other than colour-

less flat caps and grey overcoats which were always worn buttoned up to the neck. But it was more a question of style and
attitude. He wasn't a tall man. If anything he was on the short side
and he was wiry; but he had a good athletic frame and looked as if
no one could push him around. No, it was his manner that
separated him, he was like a child that behaves badly but is
unrepentant, and he had retained his hope while everyone else
despaired. He had not been crushed by life and the children's
senses responded, he touched a note of optimism in them. His
cheerfulness was infectious.

When he removed his hat she noticed that he wore a ring on his
right hand which she thought was strange. A tiny blue stone the
colour of a duck's egg caught the light when he moved. His hair
was dark, not really black, parted in the middle and slicked down
with brilliantine. Cut very short it was impossible to tell if it was
wavy or straight. There was a mixture of different smells, the
black cigarettes he smoked as he talked, casually flicking them
from a metal case; the scented smell from the stuff on his hair. She
did not know anyone else who smelt of hair scent and soap and
tobacco. It was pleasant. He must have taken a lot of care about
shaving, for his face was fresh and clear like a boy's and his teeth
and nails, far from being stained while he chain-smoked hope-
lessly, were white and clean. He was a man who took care of
himself.

'Why I was such a good friend of your family's that . . . let me
see now . . . ' the man said and screwed up his eyes while he
thought. 'Now , your grandmother . . . ' he hesitated.

'Granny Riley!' Frank burst out excitedly.

'Yeah, yeah that's her.' The man was relieved, not so much to
have remembered her name but because the old woman was
apparently still alive. 'I could tell you where she lives, or where she
lived ten years ago which must be the last time that I saw her.'

'Ten years ago!'

'Yep I've been away for that long.'

The man described their grandmother's house to the amazed
children. 'Oh I've been there many times. When I was a boy I used
to call round for Elisabeth and your granny would say 'She's not
coming out, she's practising.'

He placed his hands on his hips and sounded and looked so
much like their grandmother as he imitated her that they both
laughed delightedly.

'Oh my, I remember that cold front room of hers. The sun never came in through the window, if faced the wrong way. I reckon the only time the sun shone was early in the morning but what's the use of that? Your granny only ever unlocked that door in the afternoon, for Elisabeth to practise on the piano. That great big upright thing. She always said that they must have built the house around it because it was impossible to move. It had two brass holders for candles and some fancy open-work stuff behind the rack where the sheet music rested. Oh, and how could I forget the mother-of-pearl inlay, tiny roses on the lacquered panels! Why I always thought it was the finest piano I'd ever seen. I used to tell Elisabeth that one day I was going to get me one just like it.'

'Do you play too?'

'No, no. I wasn't going to get it for myself.'

'That's granny's piano, and she still locks the parlour door.'

'Does she? And does she still have a fan of wallpaper in the bucket by the fire grate?'

'Yes. She never has a fire there.'

'There were pictures on the walls . . . ' He glowed with the memory.

'Hey mister,' Frank said, 'did you know our dad? Were you a friend of his too? Did you know him as a boy?'

The man suddenly looked blank and older. He scratched his head and appeared to be thinking hard. Finally he looked at them. 'Your father?' he asked puzzled.

'Yeah, he died while I was still a baby. Frank wasn't even born.'

'Hmm. No I can't say I do remember your father. I don't think I ever knew him. Oh, I was away for such a long time you know that I kind of lost touch.'

'What else do you remember about gran's house then?'

The man laughed 'I remember the sofa. Ouch, how could anyone ever forget it? That big horsehair sofa that used to face the fireplace. It scratched the backs of my legs whenever I sat on it. My, the day I started wearing long pants I knew that I was a man because I could sit and listen to Elisabeth play without having to scratch. She played like an angel. Does she still?'

'Not much. Only when we're at gran's, like sometimes on Sunday.'

'Don't you live there?'

'No we live in Moses Street.'

'Moses Street? Hey isn't that where Mick Riley lives?'

'That's where we live — with Uncle Micky.'

The man looked surprised. 'You know,' he said, 'I thought that you would be with your grandmother.' He seemed to be thinking, as if he was fitting pieces of their lives together. 'Is Micky married?'

'NO!'

The man started to laugh. 'So that's how it is!' he exclaimed, 'The confirmed batchelor. We used to be great friends. I'll bet you didn't know that. We used to go away to Wales together on our bikes, and we played football for the same team. We even started our first jobs together. I remember when he first moved to Moses Street.'

The children looked at each other and grinned. He described people so accurately that they felt as though he had known them all their lives, although they had only just met.

There were only two Morgan children, Veronica and Francis her kid brother, always known as Frank. He followed her round like a puppy hanging on to everything Ronnie said or did, imitating, idolising. 'Don't call her Ronnie,' their mother always said. 'It's really pronounced Veronique you know, that's French.'

But 'Veronique Morgan' did not have the right ring about it whereas Ronnie did. So Ronnie it was, except when Mrs Morgan shouted them both for their tea — 'Veronique!' 'Francis!' — in her high voice. She was a very proud woman: it made her unpopular. She was withdrawn. A respectable widow who always wore her wedding ring.

Ronnie couldn't remember her father at all but Frank was convinced that she must have some memories because she was older than him. So she told him stories that she made up to satisfy his curiosity. She pestered her mother the way Frank did her, but Mrs Morgan did not like to speak about him. Ronnie thought it was because his memory upset her far too much and in this she was right. Mrs Morgan could not bring herself to think about her husband without her knuckles standing out white, and the dull ache in her temples starting up again.

If only she could have been a proper widow, she would have at least been at ease. A husband's death is not the wife's fault. But her predicament implied that no matter how blameless, some of the guilt was hers. For a husband to walk out on a woman meant that she had to be doing something wrong. She had been scandalised by the whole affair. Even when those who had known him well called him a scoundrel and a bad case she knew that some of this badness rubbed off onto her. Her judgement was constantly in question and, what was more, she was tied to him for life.

Sometimes she prayed that she would hear news of his death, which would free her from him. It was not because she had any idea of marrying again, no that was very far from her mind, it was just the feeling that while that man still lived she was tied to him. And then she would feel guilty for wishing his death and would confess to the priest her awful thoughts, and beg the church's forgiveness. Beyond the priest and the immediate family she told very few people, keeping her status as a widow intact.

'No Mrs Morgan, you're not lying to profit yourself but to save your children unnecessary pain, and that's different,' the priest reassured her. But she was not comforted that she lived a deception.

After he had left she had been forced to move back to her mother's because she could not afford the rent on the house. But then her brother had sent for her after the boy was born and she moved with the two children into the Dingle.

No matter how much she regretted Finbar Morgan she could never regret her kids. They were growing up into responsible, sensible beings. Lovely kids. People always commented on it. Sometimes she wondered if they were too responsible, for they had a great responsibility with only one parent. If anything happened to her, although Michael was like a father to them, they would still become as orphans. Both of them fussed over her and worried about her health. She had never been strong. Now she took cleaning jobs, night and morning. Scrubbing floors in offices down town and riding back home exhausted on the last bus.

She was never a dreamer. She did not fool herself into thinking that life would have been much better if he had stayed with them. The only difference would have been that the kids would know their father. Sometimes she wasn't even sure if that was such a good idea. They were probably better off protected by their ignorance.

Although he was a rogue he was not an idle one. He would turn his hands to anything, stupid hare-brained schemes, looking for easy money. He was in with a bad crowd. If she could have only got him away from them, he might have done all right with a bit of help. But it wasn't his way to graft and graft and quietly earn a living with a pension thrown in for good behaviour. He would rather take chances than have his life mapped out and see that it went nowhere. He liked to think big.

'Think big and talk soft,' she'd always said. But that was what had attracted her to him, the way he saw the future. He had a way with words, the gift of the blarney. She told herself that she was a fool for ever listening to him, or believing him.

Yet something in her craved the excitement he offered. Her life with him was going to be different. That was certainly true. Look at her. Two kids, deserted and never a penny from him since. And she had once had such expectations, if not for herself. What she never got over was that he hadn't even stayed long enough to see his son. It was as if he had rejected the child before he was born, rejected something he didn't know.

At first, when he had failed to return, she imagined that he had been in an accident or had got into a fight and was lying bleeding somewhere. She left Veronica with her mother and went round all the places she could usually count on him being. From one pub to another, to the betting shop, waiting outside asking the men as they came out if they had seen Finny. No one had. There was no news of him, nor ever was. As the weeks wore on the truth gradually dawned on her, but she could not accept it at first.

'You're not the first woman it's happened to,' her own mother said. 'You've got to get on with it now, and think about the baby.' She eyed her daughter's increasing waistline. 'He knew you were having another didn't he?'

Yes he had known.

She had worried that when he came back he would find the windows of their home boarded up or another family moved in, but she needn't have. And after she had given birth to Francis she felt edgy everytime someone came to the door, expecting him to turn up at the bedside and make everything all right. It was a type of bereavement that she suffered, but she could not mourn openly. She forced herself to see that he had gone for good and she condemned him for his desertion which was cowardly, leaving her to manage as best she could. Any sorrow she felt turned to bitterness as the starkness of her life stretched out in front of her, and she felt only contempt for him until gradually she grew to hate him. He had destroyed a part of her, for she had trusted him when no one else had, wanted to believe in him despite all the warnings, and her faith received a blow from which she was never to recover. She developed a cynical outlook on life, when once she had been so open and trusting. So cruelly let down.

The afternoon that the two children met the man was just like Christmas for them. Ronnie was always vague as to how it happened.

The man had told them that he was only in Liverpool for a few more days. He had been sent on business from the company in New York where he worked. As he had to sail back that very week he said that he would like to treat them. He explained, when he saw them look doubtful, that they would be doing him a favour by accepting, because their own grandmother had done so much for him when he was a boy and he always meant some day to repay her. He said that their mother would want him to. Both children looked at each other. Frank wanted guidance but Ronnie's face must have looked as confused as his.

'Look,' the man said, 'I happen to know that it's your birthday in a few weeks son, and I'd like to get you a present.'

'How do you know that?' the boy exclaimed.

The man winked. 'We have our ways. I don't quite remember the date, but I know it's around this month. Am I right?'

'Almost, it's the fifth.'

'Well, I was never very good with figures and dates but that's close enough for me. Tell you what,' he said as an idea struck him, 'why don't we go into town to that good department store. Then I can get you a birthday present and something for your sister. We can go somewhere and have some ice cream and then I'll feel I've repaid your granny just a little bit. Only you'll have to direct me, I've been away for so long that I can't remember the way. But if you lead, I can follow.'

The children jumped greedily at the chance. Ronnie always felt embarrassed at how quick they had been to take up his offer, whenever she thought back.

They led him to Lewis's. Up in the lift to the toy department where they were allowed for the first time in their lives to run riot. They could play on anything they chose to. There were toys there that they never dared imagine they might own. Ronnie had never had a proper doll in her life. She always used to say that she did not really like them. That her old rag doll was better because her gran had made it and it was soft and cuddly when she kept it in the bed at night, for it had no hard joints to dig into her. But suddenly there were rows and rows of exquisite china faces with curls and ribbons and she realised with a shock that now the possibility of owning one had opened up in front of her she had to have one. She felt that she must. She yearned for one and her small child's heart ached with love.

She was in a delightful agony of indecision, inspecting the perfect round faces and painted lashes that peered out from every box. She picked each one up and nursed it. She could actually touch and handle them. It was the closest she had ever got to any before. She could smell the strange glue and resin mixture from their wigs. There were dolls with jointed arms and legs — 'walking dolls' they were called — and there were even talking dolls that said 'mama'. No one chased her away and told her to leave them alone, because the man with his quiet air of authority was with them, walking round following, as the assistants watched from heavy lids.

Frank was as excited as his sister. If Ronnie got a doll he could play with it. He would help to dress it and she might let him comb its hair and help to tie the ribbons in. He already knew what he wanted, proper football boots with studs. He'd always wanted a pair. He thought when he was grown up he would buy himself a pair with his first week's wages, so he only glanced at the toys.

'Come on son, what do you want?'

Frank looked at his sister. Her eyes were shining with feverish excitement. 'Don't you want one of those games?' the man asked. But the boy hung back scared to look and deviate from his ideal.

'I don't want a toy,' he said and the man looked crestfallen.

'No, you see I want some football boots please. Proper ones that lace up and have studs in.'

The man's face relaxed into the broadest grin of relief.

'Oh sure, we'll go down to the shoe department right away. But first you just go right in and get yourself a toy. We'll get those boots after.'

Frank could not believe his ears. He didn't need to be told twice. He waded in among the soft toys: rows and rows of bears and squirrels, furry owls and clockwork things that moved when the key was turned. There were trucks and jeeps with wheels on spindles so that they could glide around a corner, and some had hooters that really sounded. He couldn't decide. Those trucks would make him the envy of any boy in school, but he was torn between them and a mechanical clown that did tricks on a metal bar, looping its lanky body over the pole while 'He Flies Through

The Air With The Greatest Of Ease' played from a music box in the base. Pride got the better of him and he picked up a yellow shiny car and took it to the man.

Ronnie had decided and was standing waiting as a woman wrapped up the box containing the big walking doll she had chosen. It wore a white lace dress and a little red jacket with red shoes that buttoned up. Ronnie loved the shoes, especially the little round pearly buttons that fastened up the front. But the best thing about the doll was her hair — it was straight like her own, only the doll's was cut into a fringe that hung thickly on the forehead. Her mother would never let her wear a fringe because she said that it made girls look common. But this doll was beautiful, and its thick fringe and straight hair had made Ronnie love it all the more, much more than any of the curly haired ones. Already it had become something special.

As they came down in the lift clutching their parcels they could hardly believe that this was happening. On the next floor the football boots were bought and paid for and the man bought Ronnie a pair of shoes which were all the rage then, with bows on the front. As an adult Ronnie would often recall the first time that she had gone into school wearing them. All the other girls had gathered round her and tried them on squeezing their feet into the little slippers.

The next stop was a cafe where the children were bought cake and ice cream and big glasses of lemonade. It was better than any birthday they had ever had, when they did not get any of these things.

All the time the man talked to them and asked them questions. He wanted to know as much about them as possible out of a genuine interest in them as people, it seemed to them then. He asked them what they did during the day, who their friends were, what games they played at school, what lessons they didn't like, what books they were reading. All the time he was watching them as if they were ghosts who could fade away.

'Pinch me. Any minute I'm going to wake up and you two wonderful children will be gone.'

The children laughed because they felt exactly the same. If they were to wake up not only would their friend be gone but the ice cream, the cake, the doll, the yellow car, the boots and the shoes with the bows would all vanish with him.

His eyes were never still as he talked, always looking. Seeing their features, their shabby clothes, building up a clear picture of both of them, as if he was trying to make it last a lifetime. Ronnie always said later that under his gaze they had both blossomed. She did not feel that the bare patches in her elbows were important because she was her mother's daughter and that was the best recommendation she could have. She had her mother's shining dark hair and the same eyes, the other things like smart clothes didn't matter.

In the cafe he had suddenly leaned forward and taken hold of Ronnie's hands. He just stared at them for a second and then said that she had lovely hands. Piano players fingers was what he had called the long tapering fingers that she had. He had made them all put their hands together to measure the different lengths of their fingers. 'Our hands are kinda similar,' he told Frank. 'See, we've both got these funny square nails.'

It really did seem as if the tiniest detail about them interested him. They glowed under his undivided attention. They were important with their ideas, things that their mother and uncle had no time for. He listened carefully and gave advice. He told them how to deal with bullies and what to say if someone picked on them. They did so much talking that they realised that they had never thought to ask his name or where he lived or any of the usual questions. They didn't seem to be very important then. Although they found out his name and they discovered that he worked in New York they didn't ask him anything else. It wasn't because they weren't interested, but there were questions they couldn't ask adults and, besides, it made little difference.

'Where are you from? I mean before you went to America?' Frank asked in the cafe.

'From right here,' he said tapping the table with his finger. 'Yep, right here. Same place I grew up in. But I've lived in New York for, lemme see, how old are you honey?'

'Ten and a half.'

'And I'm nearly nine.'

'Well I've lived in New York for practically the same time, nearly ten years, nine and a half I expect.'

The children laughed enjoying the comparison.

'You know this is my first time back since I went away? And when I arrived I didn't know me anybody and I didn't recognise nuthin'. But then I started walking. I had to buy me a map! And then I recognised some of the old streets, and today I got up in my hotel and I said "Finbar, you go on a walk out to the Dingle way. Go and have a look at the Cast-Iron shore.' And so I came out and who did I meet just walking about but you two, and I thought I was seeing things.'

'How did you know about us?' Frank looked confused. 'Did mother write to you?'

'An old friend who's now in America sent me out news about you son, and I'd seen photos of your sister when she was a baby.'

'Really! We're not really strangers are we?'

'No, we're not.'

Several times Ronnie thought he was about to speak but stopped himself. Later she was to dismiss this as hindsight.

Suddenly the man looked at his watch, and, remembering something, said rather shortly: 'Hey, look kids I've got to go now. I've got a meeting this afternoon at four, so I'll have to get along.' He glanced up from the gold watch and smiled as a last idea came to him.

'Hey tell me something. What are your favourite cakes? I mean your favourite favourites.'

'Eclairs!'

'Turnovers!'

'Come on,' he said and in a rush he paid the bill and ran with the children laughing out onto the street and into a baker's

'No sorry we don't have enough,' said the confused shop girl.

'Come on!' he shouted and roaring with laughter they ran out into the street.

'Where's another place?'

'Top of the street.'

'OK, charge!' and they ran behind him holding boxes and brown paper parcels wondering what on earth he was going to do.

In the shop he bought half a dozen of each cake and the perplexed assistant packed them carefully up into two boxes and tied them neatly with string.

'Here you are,' he said holding the boxes of cakes to each, 'these should keep you going for a while!'

The children shouted with laughter.

'I've really got to go now,' he said seriously.

They said nothing.

'Well I don't want your mother feeling worried about you.'

'Oh that's OK,' said Frank. 'She's not expecting us back until teatime.'

'Finbar,' Ronnie began nervously. 'Why don't you come back and say hello to mother? I know you can't come now, but before you have to return. I'm sure she'd like to thank you for all this.'

'Yes,' said Frank seizing his hand. 'Come back with us!'

For a minute Ronnie thought that she saw tears in his eyes, but he brushed his hand quickly over his eyes and they were gone.

'I can't this trip, I'm fully booked with work. This was my one afternoon free.'

'Aw why can't you come tomorrow?' Frank started to plead but Ronnie kicked him and he shut up. The man was no longer laughing. He was beginning to look uncomfortable.

'If it could be any other way I'd come back with you. I'd be proud to come back with you. You're two very special kids. But I really must go.'

'Next time?' the girl asked. 'If you have to make another trip will you see mother then?' Something about the man's face told her that she was not making a normal request.

'Next time,' was all he said. And it could have been a question — or a statement, or an answer.

He stopped a taxi and, helping them to load up, he gave five shillings to the driver. They gave him a hug like an old friend. Suddenly Ronnie said 'Do you have a message for mother?'

'Just tell her Finny says hello. Don't forget now, Finny says hello.'

They stared out of the back of the taxi waving as he stood looking after them as if there was nothing else in the world but a departing taxi with two children in it.

They never saw him again.

Whenever Ronnie remembered she always thought of it as tinged with sadness. For she had noticed how the look on the man's face had changed as the taxi pulled off. No longer laughing he looked older, mournful, bereaved. That was the word she thought of, like someone at a funeral. She hoped that he wouldn't cry, to her he was perfection and she didn't want her dream destroyed or the man turned into a ridiculous figure.

Frank could never remember that, only that they were delirious with happiness.

And the man had said 'next time'. Next time he would come and visit them. Ronnie said it wasn't like that. She knew that there wasn't going to be a next time, but neither could remember too clearly.

They walked proudly to the door from the taxi, loaded with presents and half the street came out to watch.

'Where in the name of God have you been and what have you got there?'

They tried to tell their mother, squealing with excitement, trying to out shout each other in their delight to be the one to tell the story and relate the wonderful magical events of the day.

They tore at the brown paper to show the things that they had. Their mother had become very still and quiet. She watched them, both over-excited, she saw their gorged faces. She looked coldly at the boxes of cakes.

All she said that Ronnie could recall was something about the waste. 'And he had a fine suit of clothes on him?'

'Oh yes it was lovely soft woollen stuff and he wore a ring on his finger with a little blue stone in it and a silk handkerchief . . . '

The children talked on and on. Suddenly their mother interrupted 'Go up to your beds. You've had enough excitement for one day, take those things with you.'

They looked at each other. They had expected their mother to be pleased but this resigned sorrowful look confused them.

'Oh, he said to say that Finny says hello.'

'Yes, I'm sure he does,' she said in a tired flat voice.

'Go up to bed, go on.'

They lay in the dark in the same room too excited to sleep. Even their mother's unfathomable reaction could not spoil the day for them. They would remember it for the rest of their lives. They didn't know how well they would remember it though. They didn't know that years later they would try to recall every tiny detail about the man.

Downstairs in the kitchen their mother cried and cried. Hating him more fiercely than ever before.

'Never a penny from him. Never a penny in all this time the bastard, the rotten stinking bastard. And he can throw money around like it's water. God if he ever came here I'd never have him back. Those kids need food and shoes more than once in a lifetime and he turns up and plays the big hero for the day.'

The boxes of cakes were on the table. Half a dozen eclairs and apple turnovers. Sickly fancy things, nothing that would last. That was just like him. Fancy shoes with bows indeed, when she couldn't afford a proper pair and everything came from rummage sales or hand-me-downs. He hadn't changed. He was a rogue and she'd been a fool. She swept the boxes off the table with her fists, punching savagely. 'Sod you, damn you,' she screamed and collapsed with her head in her arms, sobbing and shaking with rage.

The eclairs spilled out broken. The cream oozed onto the tiles and the apple stuff spread in a sticky puddle.

Upstairs the two children could hear their mother shouting and then the sound of sobbing.

'Why is she crying?' Frank asked feeling frightened.

'Women often cry when they're happy,' Ronnie said wondering if that was true.

'Was it because she was too happy for words that she didn't say much?'

'Yeah, must have been.'

After all, she thought as she held her dolls next to her, Finny is a very old friend. It must have been quite a shock for her.

They lay in the darkening room listening to the sound of their mother downstairs. Ronnie felt her mother's sobs as if they were in time with her breathing. She felt connected to so much happiness.

'When we're grown up will we ever cry from happiness do you think?' Frank asked.

'I don't know,' Ronnie said settling down under the covers.

She wrapped her arm around the new doll. She was going to call her Rosie. She felt sure that the old doll and Rosie would be good friends. She hugged them both and felt warm and content as her eyes began to close, and she was already half alsleep when Frank's dreamy voice murmured, 'I suppose we'd have to be very happy when we grow up and then we might.'

'Yes; very, very happy.'

'I've never heard mam sound like this,' he whispered.

Ronnie agreed. 'No, she's never been this happy before.'

New Blood

I came across my sex education indirectly via Mary's virginity which I learned about almost as soon as I could talk.

That Mary was a virgin most pure was impressed on my mind long before anyone explained what it meant. The actual word 'sex' was missing from the vocabulary of our Catholic household. What it meant, and could be used to describe, I could only glean through the hushed way bodily functions were referred to and the various parts of the body that were totally ignored, for which words, it seemed, had not been created. Sex belonged to this area of half-spoken unfinishable sentences. There was a preoccupation about it remaining absent; it was vitally important that it should not exist. Saints did not do it. Respectable people did not do it. Of what it was, I had no idea, but I came to understand that something took place between a man and a woman, something secret, to be hidden and ashamed of, something which resulted in sin.

I learnt that Mary had been spotless when her son was born and that that was a miracle. For my mother to be spotless she could not have given birth to me. I decided that I must have been adopted, the product of someone else's sin, and I would cry at night imagining that I was the child of lusty Protestants who alone could do the unspeakable whatever that gave me life.

School biology was the start to understanding, for I could not have asked my mother to fill the gaps in my knowledge, and it was not taught along with general subjects at the convent school.

'Perversion! They'll be doing it for exams next! ' my mother said about the more progressive secondary schools. But she could not be prevailed on to tell me what it was.

I studied diagrams of rabbits in cross-section and stared at the tapeworm in the jar swimming in greeny fluid.

'The tapeworm reproduces asexually: that is, it does not require a partner to . . . fertilize it.'

The virgin birth was being explained in scientific terms; some things were beginning to slot into place for me, but it took more for the picture to be completed.

I owe my adult life to Nancy Lyons, a great tall girl with striding legs and brown gym knickers who could clear the vaulting horse in one clean leap, straight off the springboard like a comet. It was she who filled me in with the mysteries of nature when I was 13.

Although Nancy had only limited knowledge and still managed to get some of that wrong, I accepted all she said in the absence of any other authority apart from the school textbook with its peculiar illustrations and odd phraseology.

At 14 I started to menstruate. I was not at all frightened because Nancy had told me that this would happen and described it accurately as it had, in fact, already happened to her. I proudly told her that I had become a woman and we went together in great glee to buy towels from the machine in the school cloakroom.

Four weeks later I was horrified to find it happening again. I rushed up to Nancy in the changing room in tears.

'You daft bugger!' she said, 'it happens every month until you have a baby, then you stop.'

'Does that mean I'm going to have a baby!' I screamed.

'Not now, it only means that you can. So you could have a baby when you get married, when you're 20, because you have to be old,' she reassured me.

When it came for the third time I was at least expecting it and resigned to the repetition of 'cycles' as Nancy called them.

'I'll have to tell my mother,' I confided in her one day. 'What am I going to say?'

Much worse than the event itself loomed my mother's possible reaction. I was convinced that it had happened so long ago to her that she had forgotten all about it and my news would come as the most awful shock, shattering the peace of her calm years.

I could not sleep. I went to Mass and prayed to God for strength and to Saint Jude for hopeless cases. I said novenas late into the night and grilled Nancy for information during the day.

'Did the Virgin Mary ever bleed like us?' I asked her.

'No, of course not.'

'Well, she had a baby didn't she?'

'Yes, but she never did the other either.'

I began to panic.

'Are you sure?'

' 'Course she didn't. Saints don't bleed. Only us lot do.'

'Does Sister Gabriel?'

' 'Course. She's a woman isn't she!'

'Yeah, but she's a nun.'

'Doesn't alter the fact that she's a woman does it?'

'Well Mary was a woman.'

'Not like you and me she wasn't. She was to be the Mother of God. Born without stain. A virgin most pure.'

Nancy gave me a knowing, worldly look.

'We 're hardly as pure as that, so we bleed.'

Simple.

'Tell your mother tonight.'

It was almost a dare.

'Bet you can't jump that fence.'

'Bet you can't hold your breath longer than 30 seconds.'

'Bet you can't tell your mother.'

This new task daunted me by its sheer impossibility, like being told to stand in a fire any length of time. If you did it to prove that you could, you were burnt to death in the process. I knew that my mother's reaction would be as fatal.

'Oh — I can't, I can't.'

Nancy, never one to recognise defeat, decided to take a different approach. Leaning forward conspiratorially she began with an obvious 'Well . . . you've got to tell her sometime.'

Then lowering her voice to almost a whisper she continued, 'She's probably worried sick that you haven't started yet. I'll bet she's thinking there's something wrong with you, that you're not growing up normal. It's your duty to tell her.'

Nancy had played her final trump card and she knew it. She sat back against the wall of the science block drawing herself up until her spine was in a straight line with the cooling bricks. I was still sprawling on the tarmac with only my shoulders propped up against the building, my school cardigan rolled up as a rough pillow between my neck and head. From her sudden upright position Nancy was oozing responsibility. She squinted her eyes and, with a critical expression, tilted back her head. She stared straight in front of her to where, in the middle distance, some first-formers were throwing a ball back and forth practising back passes and shooting. Her cool eye surveyed them as a senior, well

able to out-perform any of them, but tolerant of the next gener-
ation coming up.

Duty; she had spoken of my duty towards my mother. I had not
thought of it in such a light before. The responsibility sank in. I
was shamefaced.

'I'll tell her this evening.'

The bell rang for afternoon classes and we rose to join the
crowd of girls struggling to get into lines in the yard. The evening
was still a safe distance away as I went to my lessons, shamed by
my weakness and determined to absolve myself. I knew that I
would have to pick the right time and I knew that I would have to
get my mother on her own.

I was pondering how to do this after tea when my mother,
almost as if she had read my mind, told me to go upstairs and
change into the school frock that she had begun letting out for me,
to get me through the last hot term that dragged heavily on.

'I'll get that hem done tonight,' she said following me up.

I watched the top of her head reflected in the full-length mirror
as she knelt at my feet pinning up the skirt. Still I hesitated. It
would be dangerous to say anything now I told myself, her mouth
was full of pins. When she took them out, when she said something . . . then I would tell her. I paced myself. Uncannily she
removed them.

'Will you stop fidgeting for Christ's sake!' she said.

When she got round to my knees. I was delaying again.

'Look, I've warned you!'

She had spoken twice, I had missed my cue. I had to begin
somewhere. I stared up at the ceiling — it's now or never. All
right, after three.

One, two, three . . . I opened my mouth.

One, two, three . . . words failed me.

Why was I such a coward?

One, two, three . . .

'They're lousy sports in the upper school you know. The B team
particularly. They play really dirty netball. They always move
when they're holding the ball, and they shove defence out of the
way, which you're not allowed to do you know.'

'Uh huh hmm,' my mother said, continuing to pin up the stiff
yellow material.

This was dreadful. I wasn't getting to the point at all.

'At the last inter-form tournament one of the fourth's defenders nudged the goalpost so that our shooter missed. They didn't even get penalised for it. It's really not fair — and I started my periods. I don't like playing against a side that cheats,' I wound up quickly, knowing that she had heard me because she pricked her expert fingers and sat back on her heels staring up at me with a look of terror on her face, her finger in her mouth sucking blood.

Without a word she got up and left me imprisoned in the pinned frock, unable to move without scratching my knees, staring uneasily into the mirror. I wondered if the shock had been too much for her. Would she faint?

I heard her walk along the landing into her bedroom and the sound of rummaging, of drawers being opened, searched through. Looking for smelling salts or holy water. But when she came back into the room she was carrying neither; instead she held out a dusty navy-blue packet.

'Here,' she said, 'use these.'

The precious parcel passed from her to me. The paper was faded, bleached to a dull blue in places, the way things go after spending too much time in a shop window. It cracked as I opened it, tearing easily. Inside were snowy white towels, much larger than the ones I got from the school cloakroom. They were so different that I stared at them, prodding their cotton wool softness with my finger. They were luxurious, special.

I did not know then, but she had no further use for them, never would. They were souvenirs of her fertility, bought years ago. Sacred relics now being transferred. She looked embarrassed as she gave away the last traces of her childbearing years.

'Use these' was all she had said as the parcel went dryly between us. Bloodless, waiting for new blood.

She knelt back in her original position and continued pinning up my skirt in silence.

This story first appeared in *Spare Rib* no. 132

The Water's Edge

When the alarm began to screech it was still dark. The figure sleeping did not respond until the fourth or fifth repeat, when a hand was flung out to stop the mechanism. The feet stung as they came into contact with the icy floor, while on the face a sensitive muscle caused puckering around the mouth as eyes shut tight and nostrils widened to draw in air.

As a small child back in Ireland she used to make the same expression when she felt the cold that seeped up between the stone flags. Quite early on she had learnt to recognise the difference between the physical chill and the cruel cold from the bogland that had lain in the peat for centuries preserving its character.

This type of cold is more bitter, rawer, for it froze the blighted potato, it crippled the cottage weavers bent double at their looms, it howled in the flax-retting pools and later in the factories where the green linen was worked. It blows now around hedge and thatch and ruined churchyard, along low stone walls and the water's edge. The very same cold that her grandmother felt while bent at the range, coaxing heat from the single clod of turf, had later been felt by her own mother, despite electricity, for it rose through and conquered.

Eileen stood up in the room and drew her dressing gown tight against the physical cold; there was no easy protection from the other. It followed her, hunting her spirit. Sometimes on all fours crawling from the soft spongy ground of Tirconell, moist with the earth still clinging. Other times, blowing as wind, it wrapped itself chill and damp around her. It was at its strongest when she was alone.

She opened the door and shivered as she flicked on the light to peer along the landing. Under the bare bulb the passage appeared

119

tinged with green, mould was setting in. There were no signs of life from the other boarders.

'Thank God,' she prayed as she went along the corridor to the bathroom.

It meant that Michael was on the late shift again. When he worked sociable hours she was always nervous in case they should run into each other on the stairs. It worried her that they might be seen one day, both in their nightclothes out on the landing and, despite the voice of common sense which told her that she owed no one excuses for honest behaviour, she continued to be troubled by the picture of the two of them.

Michael drank occasionally. Some nights when he came back the worse from it he talked about the 'auld country' but it was always in the past and it made Eileen sad to listen. She hated being in the kitchen when he returned like that. Those were the nights when he would coax the landlady to take a wee sup of whisky with him. She would giggle like a schoolgirl as she fetched sugar and hot water.

Michael's emotions embarrassed her, but more than that; his voice propelled her into a place that was cold and empty, where they were all alone. She hated that place, hated Michael for implying that that was where they would all end up. It was different for her because she was young and everything was temporary, but for him, there could be no excuse of transition. He was still there after all that time; the reserves he had meant to build up he had not managed. He had nothing, in fact, except loneliness and the continual cold. Things which had grown up easily over the years where nothing else would.

She turned on the tap. Some greenish brown liquid sputtered from the tank. Cold. The pilot had gone out.

'The Devil' she cursed. 'I'm not going all the way to the kitchen for matches, the Constant Mystery will be in here when I get back. I must remember to keep my own box.'

Having decided to perform her ablutions in cold water, she set about them quickly. Taking the tube of toothpaste from her dressing-gown pocket, she pressed, from the bottom, barely enough to cover her brush and began cleaning her teeth vigorously. The exercise brought her face to life, the blood in her veins moved.

She rinsed her mouth and spat apologetically into the sink.

There was blood for the sins of the world.

The sliver of coal-tar soap would not lather, but her hands rubbing against her face created another little feeling of warmth. She washed away the mark of original sin with the baptismal water and, as the towel was damp and grey, she used her dressing-gown to dry it.

On the way back to her room she practised the technique that she was developing to keep her feet away from the cold floor. It was a sort of hopping step that brought only the smallest part of the ball of her foot into contact with the floor for the shortest length of time. This gave her sufficient spring to be able to cross a large expanse of lino before becoming earthbound. She thought it was a little like floating only that, she imagined, would be a more sustained motion.

As she reached her door the Constant Mystery who lived across the landing was coming through hers. She was the other boarder. Mrs Hennessey did not know what to make of her.

'She's been with me for almost four years now,' she said one day to Eileen, 'and I still don't know what she does with herself. She can't work, not with the times she gets up in the day. Sometimes she lies in bed until after four, may God strike me down if I lie I've heard the springs of her bed creaking while I've been cooking the tea.'

Eileen did not require such proof, for as the kitchen was under the Mystery's room, it seemed highly probable that every move she made was anxiously listened for, if only out of concern that she had not ceased breathing.

'No one can lie in bed that long,' Mrs Hennessey said. 'Not without there being something wrong.'

She told Eileen that the Mystery, in her youth, had been a concert pianist and had toured all round America before the arthritis got to her. It was rumoured that she had been engaged to a cellist with the Hungarian Philharmonic Orchestra that she had met in New York, but had broken it off because he was Jewish or a bigamist.

'Well its the same thing isn't it?' Mrs Hennessey had related. 'They can have more than one wife.'

Whatever the truth was, a portly woman in her late fifties was coming out of the room over the kitchen, wearing a black silk kimono. Her orange hair grated violently with the green pallor of the corridor and her skin hung loose and white like so many bandages. Eileen quickly shut her door, grateful for the haven of her room.

Only one bar worked on the electric fire. It scorched a pink strip of flesh under her knees as she stood combing her hair. Everywhere else she was cold.

The cold would not let her sleep at night. It blew under the door, took shape and crawled up onto her bed, kept her awake by singing to her, whistled from the corners of her room and left mud everywhere. It always found her.

She began to pull her clothes on furiously.

Eileen had originally come to London to be a nurse like her elder sister, but on the boat coming over she kept thinking how other people's blood made her sick. By the time the boat docked all she saw were open wounds and yards and yards of gauze dressing. Brigid was shocked by her appearance when they met at Euston.

'What in God's name is wrong with you?' she had asked. Eileen, in a panic, could only sob that she had changed her plans.

That night she stayed in a hotel by the station and the next day moved into a hostel. Brigid wrote to their mother from the nurses' home. Eileen thought that she might take the news better if it did not come directly from her. Their mother was one of the sensitive types who let external events peel away at their internal fibre. Her stomach lining must have been a transparent tissue of veins by now which each day grew clearer as the acid anxiety etched deeper upon the gossamer membranes.

Eileen was said to have inherited her mother's constitution.

When she was a child the sight of a hen with its neck wrung was enough to turn her stomach, and there had been her illness when she had spent a long time lying on her back in the convent. She remembered only snatches of that time.

White veils.

Nuns' habits that crumbled and collapsed without substance when she reached out to touch them.

There was a crucifix. It would spin very fast until it became a silver point of light. Some days it moved around the walls of the room, others it just hung limply, often upside down.

She remembered disjointed conversations with people whose faces disappeared and reassembled as they spoke, with their features in all the wrong places.

Black and white was for the priest, blue and white for the Immaculate Conception.

They lit candles, little votive lamps in red glass. Red for the blood that was being shed.

The nuns had given her a miraculous medal which she still wore around her neck. Reflected in the mirror its French inscription was going backwards.

She thought how Brigid had really taken care of her when she had first arrived. She had found the advert of Mrs Hennesseys in the *Irish Newsletter* and urged her to go to the address in Kentish Town; and she had showed her round London. Sundays in Regents Park, or Hampstead Heath, 'looking for the bits of green' she had said. Eileen thought it was a shabby green, a pale watery tone, and it had made her feel homesick. There was enough of it back there without chasing for it everywhere and she had wanted to see the Palace and Westminster and Tower Bridge, all the *gombean*[1] things. At home the green had made her eyes feel like they were trembling in their sockets. If she stared hard at it and closed her eyes, all she saw was red. Here she saw only black spots.

'Forgive us our trespasses as we forgive those that trepass against us and lead us not into temptation but deliver us from evil . . . '

Praying gradually took over her thoughts. It was a nervous habit. While some people bit their nails, Eileen prayed.

She knew that if she did not hurry she would miss breakfast and perhaps be late for work again. She did not want the manageress to have any further reason for being unpleasant to her beyond her usual level of ill-humour, which came from somewhere inside herself, or so it appeared to Eileen.

'She isn't a Catholic either.'

It was a feeble excuse for condemning the woman but she made it, gulping greasy tea and cold bacon. Our Lady was partial.

'Are we to judge others because of their failings when all men are sinners?'

This was not only the voice of reason talking. Eileen knew and shivered.

'You must learn from the manageress's example, as she will from yours.'

Eileen's guilty example dragged itself before her.

'You were late twice last week, is it any wonder that she becomes . . . unpleasant . . . and . . . you stole a biscuit from the confectionary stand.'

Eileen smarted. She had known that Our Lady would mention that, she had been waiting for it from Tuesday when the incident occurred, until then, with guilt mounting.

'I didn't really steal it. The packet was split when I was restocking the shelves and we always share out damaged goods for break-time.'

'That has nothing to do with it. To whom did that packet of biscuits belong?'

'Well, the supermarket I suppose.'

'Was there or was there not a price on it at which the article in question could be purchased?'

'Twenty three pence, they were on offer.'

'And did you in any way attempt to pay for the item?'

'But who to?'

'The supermarket, the manageress, Mr Quicksave.'

'But things are always getting smashed. Broken biscuits turn up all the time in the staff room, it's quite common practice, the manageress wouldn't have taken the money for them.'

'So, you follow the example of a shop full of thieves. Poor Mr Quicksave, no wonder the shop is running at a loss,' said the Lady sadly.

Eileen felt ashamed. Her soul bore the sin of theft. Guilty, guilty.

She had a brainwave.

'I'll put the money in the till . . . ' But what if somebody saw her doing it? Then they might think that she really was stealing and the till would be out at the end of the day. Despair.

'Put the money in the church missionary box,' prompted the voice.

'Yes,' she beamed, 'and I'll not eat anything else that gets damaged.'

The Lady smiled at her. Eileen radiated goodness, she was saved.

'Forgive me Gentle Mother, I'll try not to sin again. Jesus Christ! is that the time? I have to run.'

'Will you be in at the usual time?' shouted Mrs Hennessey from the kitchen.

Eileen stopped on her way out. 'Well today is Friday. Late

Night. I'll be in just after seven.'

No matter how often the landlady was told, she always forgot that Eileen worked two hours later on a Friday and her tea was always waiting dried up and tepid, in the oven.

'I didn't realise,' Mrs Hennessey said every Friday, serving the ruined meal.

It was her weekly penance. Ever since the church had abolished 'meat on Fridays' she had struggled to devise something personal to replace it with. This stopped her having to think about it. In a way she was almost grateful.

'I expect you'll be in a hurry. Going out are you?'

Eileen knew that question meant there would not be any pudding.

'Yes,' she sighed. 'I'm going out.'

'God bless you dear.'

'Good morning.'

It took about ten minutes to walk to work, so she felt all the worse for being late. She arrived breathless.

'Hail Mary full of grace the Lord is with thee . . . ' she panted, armed with the knowledge the Immaculate Conception had given her over breakfast that they were all examples, they had all been planted.

She was stacking packets of frozen peas into the freezer, her fingers went numb. Saint Brendan in his little leather boat was bobbing westwards amongst the ice floes on his way to the new continent. He left his monastery to seek out God's Kingdom. Eileen was humbled.

'Me bloody hands have gone dead,' Sheila said to her. She had nodded agreement, but had not complained.

In the afternoon she was moved to tinned fruit re-stocking and labelling with a gun. She shot tin after tin. *Quicksave* were selling dead cling peaches with bullets in their brains. 53 pence, got you! 53 pence, take that!

Their screams echoed in the warehouse upstairs. The tiles ran red in fruit syrup.

'Aren't you finished yet?' the supervisor called over.

'I'm almost,' she shouted. 'Just a half dozen or so to go.'

At the sound of her voice, three women who had been talking by one of the tills turned to look at her. Their faces were a mixture of surprise and indignation.

Eileen was getting used to it. She was a human being until she opened her mouth. As soon as she spoke her identity revealed itself. She was crawling on all fours through turf, it clung to her, sucked her down. She was dragging a corpse behind her when it began to sing high and sharp. There was wind screaming for the dead in every corner of her room. It would not let her sleep at night. She was cold, cold as death; there was blood on her hands, guilty, guilty.

The Trinity stared at her. Guilty, guilty, they said.

She had seen the headlines, heard the radio. She knew the word murderer she had learnt the words 'terrorist', 'extremist'. IRA, UVF, UDA was a chant in her head.

For the rest of the day at work she said little. Too scared to open her mouth and unleash such horrors. One phrase from her alone would conjure up images of violence, vivid and bloody, and she had other things to occupy her mind rather than visit such distress on people by the mere sound of her voice. She was dangerous with her gift of speech so she worked silently, letting everything resume its normal path.

Back in her room she opened a packet of tights and laid her clothes out on the bed. The skirt was very straight with a slit to her thigh. 'By God, but that's slit up to your neck. It's a whore they'll be taking you for. You'll be crippled with rheumatism. Me children'll have me destroyed, I'm kilt, kilt.'

'Oh shut up!' Eileen snapped, and her mother disappeared. The *sean bhean bhoct*[2] wept in the corner in a black shawl. Eileen was making up.

Her father used to shout about what he called painted women, but Eileen and her sisters had carried on outlining their eyes.

The old woman wrung her hands over the corpse and began to *caoin*[3]. Eileen shivered.

The men of Ulster were low with their pangs, five days and four nights the curse of Macha[4] upon them. Weak as women in their labour. Who dared to shed their blood now would suffer from the same affliction.

There was no blood in the corpse. They pierced the side and out came only water, cold, cold.

She spat and coaxed her eye lashes into black spikes with mascara. Green eye shadow, wet fields with black crows sitting. The sun was setting, she caught it with hair lacquer. She made herself ready for when Conchobhar[5] would call her to enter his bed. Unlike proud Deirdre, she would have as many children as God willed.

The cheap gilt earrings caught the light as she shut the door and ran lightly down the stairs. She shivered slightly as she reached the street. Alone in the room the old woman pulled the shawl around her shoulders, biding her time.

NOTES

1. *Gombean* gaimbim — to profit by usury or taxation. A corrupted form used as a term of abuse to mean stupid or foolish.

2. *Sean bhean bhoct* (pron. shān vān vōkt) — poor old woman. The reference is to the old woman of Beara who is older than Ireland itself and renews her youth time and time again. Much of Ireland is said to owe its existence to her. In some tales she is Ireland.

3. *Caoin* (pron. keen) ag caoineadh — to cry. Traditional mourning undertaken by women to prevent the deceased's spirit re-entering the body.

4. *Macha* appears in different guises and it is thought that she was a survival of a mother goddess worshipped in Ireland prior to the arrival of the Celts. In the Ulster Cycle of the legend she appears as the wife of Crunniuc, a farmer. Against her will while pregnant, she was forced to race the King's horses. Although she won the contest, she lost her life giving birth to twins immediately after. Before her death she uttered a curse on the men of Ulster (warriors) for having no compassion. For nine generations after, the men were visited with birth pangs lasting for nine units (noinden). This affliction would occur during the times of their greatest difficulties, for example before a battle, and the province was defended entirely by the women and young boys during these times.

5. *Conchobar* (pron. cŏnōvar) was one of the Kings of Ulster. He took *Deirdre* as a baby after hearing it prophesied that she would grow into the most beautiful woman in Ireland, and had her brought up, away from any men, until she was ready to be his wife. Deirdre escaped, however, and took a lover. Her fate after recapture was to live with Conchobar and the man who had slain her lover 'as a sheep between two rams'. While being driven in a chariot from one man to the other, she put out her head and smashed it against a standing stone rather than endure such a life.

Prize Giving

They were proud anxious parents. She, nervous and fidgety in a grey coat. He, inarticulate, choking on pride. Their pride was the one thing that was holding them together, tying up the nerve ends with a certainty, for they were sure of their daughter. Their anxieties were for themselves.

She looked down at herself. Her bust was too big and her back too narrow. The shoulder seams of her coat drooped too much around the arms, loose and ungainly while the buttons strained over her chest. She did not fit into her clothes. The lines of her body were not well tailored. There was always something too big or too small or too long. She wore a large diamante brooch over her left breast and wondered if it was a mistake. The more she thought about it, the more awkward it looked, pinned on, the size of a dinner plate. It caught her eye unashamedly like a crude trophy, drawing attention to her. She did not want attention, especially there! She was not proud of herself, she would have preferred to sink out of sight. Her hand reached up and quickly unpinned the clasp. She shut it and stowed it carefully in her pocket. After that she felt safer and the feeling of pride for Siobhan engulfed her again. She and her husband rose on peaks only to crash from pleasure to nervousness, pride to terror.

He was unable to speak. He was scared that the words would come out backwards when he tried to talk or he would say the wrong thing. Sentences always went askew in his mouth. As long as he had been in England words were his master, calling the tune to the graceless dancer. Sometimes when he heard himself talking his voice sounded so hesitant, so unsure, that it was bitter for him to try to listen. He had been good at school (his wife agreed that Siobhan took after him), he had been confident and knew the right answers; but that was a long time ago. He lost his nerve. Now, when he was worried about using the wrong word or tense, he would leave them out altogether rather than make a mistake. Tonight he was dumb with fear.

She linked her husband's arm to hold herself up. She could not let Siobhan down tonight. All the way to the hall she was scared of falling over with her weak ankle and wished that she had not worn the shoes with those stupid heels to make her taller, for they made her legs look so much thinner. She felt all unbalanced; heavy and solid on top, tapering to a point where her feet should have been. She looked down at the wasted muscles in her calves and the delicate floriate vein that had first blossomed when she was pregnant and had stayed, faded now into a finely drawn root. If she let go of his arm she would go down like a bowling skittle. She hoped that she would not get mud all over her stockings.

'Don't walk so fast,' she pleaded.

'Fast! he thought ironically. When he owed it to his child to be a youthful playing parent he got breathless with his weak heart and had to gasp apologies. Walks together were torture, Siobhan wanted to run everywhere or to skip. And now his wife was asking him to slow down.

'We'll be late, we'll miss the start,' he said and he tightened his grip on her arm to support her and pull her along.

To arrive late meant that all heads would turn to watch, giving them disapproving glances as they shuffled looking for their seats. He could already hear their errant footsteps echo in the sepulchral chamber of the hall. Disgraceful. Like turning up drunk to a funeral. He would do anything to avoid eyes on him; creep in in the dark if he could, quietly softly, to disappear, extinguished by the house lights. *Nosferatu* of the stalls.

Neither of them could bear up to inspection. They were too old to be Siobhan's parents. This bright shining child had been a blessing too late in their lives. The gap in age seemed to widen, not close, as Siobhan grew older and sometimes they thought that they could see envy in her for the youthful families her friends belonged to, while her own parents aged visibly. In a metal box under their bed she kept worn brown photographs of young men and women in full bloom, lost generations of family, the blue grey death certificates in a tight wedge, musty with the smell of damp, stale when the lid was lifted. Their marriage certificate lay folded neatly. Their birth certificates were all together. His, faded and torn, the writing barely legible as the ink had worn to the dullest grey. The Irish harp still stood out nobly on a green ground. Here was the pink and yellowed certificate cracking like dry skin.

PLACE OF BIRTH . . . . . Liverpool

FATHER'S OCCUPATION . . . . . Carter

MOTHER'S SIGNATURE . . . An X

ADDRESS . . . . Clancy's Boarding House, Hunter Street.

She was English by an accident. They skitted her about it back in Mayo — because she was so pale.

''Twas the English air,' her mother always said.

The date on her birth certificate seemed to grow larger, more entrenched with age.

'Surely that can't be right,' she had thought, genuinely shocked, the last time she had looked at it before stowing it away, back out of sight but not mind, into the darkness of the cold box. That was where they both belonged, somewhere out of sight where they would not be an embarrassment to their daughter.

They sat in at night; Siobhan doing homework, always reading always studying. In the corner the television showed them pictures of ideal families selling toothpaste and cornflakes, laughing with perfect teeth. They became comfortable in their seclusion.

They used to go out. When they were courting they went dancing. Saturday nights were spent at the Grafton Ballroom covered in moving flecks of light from the crystal ball and the feel of the smooth waxed floor underfoot. She remembered the smell of brillantine on the neatly combed hair of her partners as she stepped out with them to take the floor. She had been a fine careful dancer in those days, but he had the two left feet of a ploughboy and only danced on sufferance. She enrolled him for a course of lessons at Billy Martin's school of dancing but he said he felt embarrassed walking round a room counting 'one two three turn, one two three turn,' and everyone going in different directions. When she married him the dancing stopped. They had few excursions out together. He was not a drinker and although she would not have liked him to go off on his own and come in late smelling of beer and urine like her own father used to, she would nonetheless have enjoyed an occasional trip to the pub. But the more they hid themselves the more difficult it was to break their habits.

When they arrived at the hall there were already groups of people standing around outside in loose gatherings, talking comfortably together, recognising old acquaintances. Glossy, poised and perfect toothed. He felt her hold his hand as the courage drained out of him. Were they the only couple who did not know anybody?

The doors of the foyer were wide open to the street on such a fine summer's evening. His vision swam in the yellow light travelling from the sleeping docks out across the waterfront. It spread over the city bathing everything from the warehouses to the neat new council flats, mushrooming around the industrial estate, in a golden gleam of prosperity. At the Pier Head night-workers waited for the factory buses to take them out for their shifts, while in the distance, but never too far away, the dark slump was baying as it steadily advanced.

At the top of Brownlow Hill the cranes stood out against the skyline. The foundations for the new cathedral had been laid and the first stage of building was over. The crypt was finished, white walled and modern.

'We talk with an accent exceedingly rare,
Meet under a statue exceedingly bare,
And if you want a cathedral
We've got TWO to spare,
In my Liverpool home.'

The audacity of the people, changing the words of the song before it was even finished! He wondered if he would see it in his day. The Anglican cathedral was still not complete after all that time. Cathedrals would not be rushed. At least the Anglicans had built theirs to look like a church, somewhere to go and pray in. The plans for theirs made it look like a space rocket. It would be like going to mass at a launching site. The Orange Lodge were going to have a bloody field day, he thought.

'Well, serves us right.'

He ached trying to move with the times, but how could he when it all got so fast like an uphill rush? His ecumenism was the sort that would live and let live as long as he was not expected to change. He did not mind the idea of Siobhan playing mixed games with a C of E school as long as she was safely back on the school bus to her own Catholic classroom at the end of it.

He felt he had lived all his life by divisions. His own country was divided. The boundary around the North may have just been a red line drawn on maps, but it made it into a different world. The people like goldfish that swelled or shrank according to their habitat, had become diverse. There was something about the set of the eyes of the Ulster Irish, a world-weary thing. His mother used to tell the old story of how Fintan from the seat of Tara had allocated all things to the separate provinces when Ireland was divided up. To the North was bequeathed conflicts and assaults, so that Ulster should be ever battle-scarred and torn. He knew it was just a matter of time before it would all flare up again like the rising in the South. Now he lived in a divided city, torn by religion, its peoples needing two football teams for their different loyalties. It annoyed him when he saw the message on the wall changed to read 'God bless our Popeye'. It hurt him to see how little respect there was between them. The white walled monument rising from the rubble where the workhouse had once stood was important to him.

'This is the first time,' he told Siobhan,' that two Cathedrals will face each other, recognising the other's existence and bowing with dignity.' Deep down he feared that theirs would not look half as dignified.

Every year the school hired the Philharmonic Hall in the city centre for prize giving. It was a prestigious affair aimed at attracting new pupils and satisfying the governors. A local dignitary, a chaplain who had found fame on the missions, or someone else of note, was often cajoled into giving a speech. Sometimes a past pupil who had done well was invited back to present the prizes and the audience was always swelled by the Old Girls Commission which made a point of turning up every year. It was one of the better girls' schools in Liverpool. Generations of schoolgirls passed down through families from mother to daughter, instilling a sense of loyalty to the establishment. Moist eyes always greeted the school song, the gracious Alma Mater.

The choir rehearsed all year for its annual exposure and the band was keyed into shape. Uniforms had to be pressed and cleaned ready for the night and the costumiers in Bold Street worked overtime getting the colours sewn into black robes and unpacking mortar boards in time to let the smell of camphor fade.

She had starched Siobhan's blouse and ironed it and steamed the box pleats in the gymslip between brown paper. She hated that gymslip. As soon as the skirt was sat on the pleats went out of shape. It was such an impractical uniform she thought, and there was so much of it too! She had been horrifed when the euphoria of Siobhan's scholarship had worn off and she reckoned what it was worth in hard cash. There was a uniform grant, but he would not let her apply for it and risk shaming themselves.

The inventory of uniform still haunted her. It was so long and there were so many different items . She thought that there were enough clothes to last a life time.

WINTER UNIFORM
4 cream shirts
1 brown and yellow tie
1 brown gymslip
2 cardigans with yellow piping
A greatcoat
A brown tailored machintosh
1 brown corduroy jockey cap
1 brown and yellow scarf
1 pair of brown gloves
2 pairs of thick brown woollen tights
fawn hose
brown lace-up outdoor shoes
brown leather indoor shoes (slipperette variety)

SUMMER UNIFORM
3 yellow cotton dresses
2 belts
1 brown blazer
1 straw boater with brown trim
3 pairs of white kid gloves
light summer shoes (fawn or brown, no heels)
white ankle socks or nylons

GAMES UNIFORM
1 pair divided skirts
2 airtex shirts
2 pairs white towelling socks
1 pair of white plimsols
1 pair of track shoes
tennis whites/skirt & blouse or fitted dress

The worst part about it was that everything had to be ordered from the gents' tailors in town. There was no way anything cheaper could be substituted. Even the blouses had to be a special off-white creamy colour that was difficult to copy. A white shirt from a department store at a fraction of the price would have made Siobhan stand out, gleaming in her cheap shirt. The list recommended four as a minimum. She had bought two and washed one every night. The games uniform seemed totally unnecessary to her. Why did it require such a special outfit just to play hockey in and chase balls around a field? Siobhan had to have long divided skirts with inverted pleats that had to be sent to the dry cleaners every fortnight. A tennis racquet and a case, a briefcase, a good fountain pen, a geometry set, mapping pens and a ruler, coloured pencils, two and a half yards of cotton material for needlework, a sewing case . . .

They had thought that it would never end.

And the demands from the school never did. It was always the same. Give generously, give something. Gifts to be raffled, objects for the sale of work, food for the Christmas hamper, cakes for the cake stall. One event would no sooner be over than another took its place and whether it was money for the missions or the school trip to Chester she had ceased to notice. She knew that there would be no end to it. It was the same at church. The collection boxes full of copper and the parish priest angry.

Inside the hall girls were already filling up the stage. They came pouring out of concealed entrances in a flood of brown and yellow school colours to take up their positions on the seating arrangement that curved in a huge semi-circle as far as the eye could see.

The stage was tiered, with a flat area usually kept for the concert pianist or soloist. Visiting orchestras played there and massed choirs of Welshmen. Brass band ensembles in spotless military uniforms that they hung in polythene bags inside the coach as soon as they had finished, even the odd rock concert had graced the boards.

Now a hush fell over the audience as teachers wearing their annual colours around their shoulders walked solemnly onto the stage, parading their qualifications. They formed a black fringe at the front while green, white, lilac, gold, the erudite colours bobbed. Inside the programme, against the names, were the titles — lists of letters that meant nothing to her. She wondered if she could manage to peep from the corner of her eyes to get a look at the woman on her left to check that she was not doing anything wrong.

In the boxes and the good seats at the front, sat the VIPs and distinguished people. She wondered what their connection was with the school. They could not all have been parents singled out for favour, besides, there were too many priests among them. She felt as if she had the least right to be there. What did it matter that one of those girls was her daughter? She had handed Siobhan over to the greater institution of education.

Everyone stood up. She jumped, terrified of being slow. The headmistress was walking on stage, regal in her sweeping black habit. With a gracious gesture she showed her distinguished visitors their seats and sat down giving the cue for everyone else to sit. The staff sat, then the girls a fraction behind them. She hoped that there would not be too much getting up and sitting down. She glanced at her husband. He had found Siobhan out of the rows of faces and was smiling peacefully.

'Sixteenth row up on the right, five seats in from the centre aisle.'

She fished in her handbag for her distance glasses.

'Where? Where?'

He pointed.

'Yes,' she nodded having seen nothing.

'Look at this,' He pointed towards the programme.

She took her distance glasses off and put her reading glasses back. She hated him because he could use bifocals. The time she had tried she thought that the floor was coming up to meet her all the time and could not place her feet without worrying. She thought that cars 400 yards away were actually on top of her and had to be helped across the roads.

He pointed to one of the names, light shining on his glasses. It was one of the teaching nuns.

'Look,' he said. 'She must be very intelligent,' and indicated with his forefinger the parade of the alphabet after her name.

Someone immediately in front turned around to look at the clock on the back wall and he coloured, imagining that they had heard him pronounce judgement. He was impressed by any outward signs of learning, and having bowed to superior knowledge found himself unable to straighten up again.

After the choir had sung various arrangements and the band had performed a scratching fugue, the guest, a young priest who had worked in the Congo, gave a speech, urging the girls to look to the reverend mother as an example of womanhood to which they should aspire. She nodded coyly, acknowledging the compliment with a graceful wave of her hand. Then she read her annual report which told of the activities the school had engaged in, the trophies they had won, the number of university entrances they had gained. They could not afford to lose one benefactor or one endowment grant. 'Look,' the report was saying, 'we are worthy of maintaining. Help to keep us afloat this year and the next . . . '

The list of prizes was being read out and the girls began to clamber down from the back of the stage to troop out and shake hands with the priest and listen to his polite congratulations. And in the middle of it was their daughter. Distinction . . . special merit . . . something or other . . . it was all a gabble to them in which the only clear thing was their child's face. Their child accepting effortlessly the warm approval of these people.

She had walked onto the stage as if she had been born to do so, slowly, taking her time. She had even turned a calm smile on the audience before returning to her seat. He thought that Siobhan had taken longer than the others had to get back to her place. She seemed to be so long on the stage, hovering, enjoying the controlled applause and hot lights. If it had been him, well, he would have run, kept his head down until he was out of the way. All those English people staring at him!

But Siobhan looked around as if she wanted to look into everyone's face and let them know that she was not scared of anyone. The hall, the school, the prizes, all belonged to her and she was at home, her confidence soaring to the upper gallery.

Sometimes he could not understand how Siobhan was their daughter. Her ways were so very different. She was so English, a foreigner to her parents. To her, Mayo was just a postmark on a card from cousins she did not know very well. If she ever brought friends home for tea he noticed how his wife grew nervous in case she did something wrong like pour the milk in first or forget to put out a jug, so that they could all tell that usually they poured straight from the bottle. She would become flustered and forget the forks, or drop things on the floor.

Siobhan saw everything and probably made excuses for her mother back at school. And when he thought that his own father had taken his teeth out to eat and set them on the table beside him. Siobhan would have been sick. Perhaps it was lucky that she had never known her grandfather, the way she complained about him for making noises when he ate. She said she could not bear it. She was sensitive and their grossness insulted her. He wondered what she said about him. Did she apologise for his accent, translate? He remembered the school elocution lessons; compulsory the letter from school had said and she had come home from them saying that they said things wrongly and correcting their speech with clipped vowels.

'RARSEBREE jam,' she had asked for in the cafe. He had nearly died.

'Go and ask for it yourself,' he had told her.

'You are saying that backwards,' she often told him with a look of disdain when he forgot and used the Irish construction. Am I not? Can I not? Amn't I?

'Are you taking Siobhan to school?' his wife would ask and he would forget the easy English way, that he could just say yes or no.

'I'm taking her,' he would reply.

'Why do you always answer a question by repeating it?' Siobhan asked him crossly. 'It sounds so silly.'

Not like the French, he thought. Exotic they were. Now having a French father, that would be something. Nice flowing way they have of talking, like they're singing, soft gentle sound of words. *Doucement, lentement, la vie en rose.* Not like the Irish, *nach bhfuil sé fliuch, nach bhfuil sé salach.** Eck, eck in the throat. Sounds like phlegm.

'Jesus Mary and Joseph!' was all he ever swore in English. 'Holy Mother of God! May the saints protect us!' Each time he lost his temper he called down a blessing not a curse.

'You sound like one of those comedians on tv,' she had said.

At the reception later, there were parents shaking hands and congratulations flowing. Their child across the room was

---

* *nach bhfuil sé fliuch* (pron. nack wilshe fluck)—isn't it wet? *nach bhfuil sé salach* (pron. nack wilshe salack) — isn't it dirty?

laughing with some friends while her parents stood in a little patch of silence. But eventually it had to happen. He went up with her coat, loving, holding it open, not knowing how he was going to interrupt, he hardly dared speak.

Siobhan did not see him, she kept talking while he hovered behind her shoulder, his smile wearing him out. Gingerly he tapped her elbow.

'Come on young lady, time to leave — bid goodnight to your acquaintances.' Formal tortured speech like he had heard in the films.

He thought that he ought to help her into her coat like he had seen the men do, even James Cagney in the re-runs.

Villains held coats open, gangsters waiting for their molls.

'Come on young lady,' he repeated, wanting to help her with her coat.

Siobhan snatched it from him crossly. She blushed and put it on herself. Even she knew that certain things just were not done. Honestly, in front of her friends too! He thinks he's putting a mink wrap on her as they leave a nightclub. They had seen the same films on Sunday afternoons together. Silly old fool! You don't do that for a child!

The unspoken words rang in his head. 'I knew you would make a show of me,' as her eyes filled with hot angry tears.

Her father's gaze showed hurt, he had started to panic and she had to look away from him not wanting to see the pain in his face. She pretended it had not happened, but her friends had fallen silent, embarrassed. When she turned back she hoped he would be gone. Then her mother crossed over to where they stood knowing something was wrong. Why was he standing so stiffly, the life gone out of him and look at Siobhan, ignoring him!

'I'll slap you young madam,' she said angrily while a low moan escaped from him.

'Oh God. Not here!' and he turned and walked out down the flight of red-carpeted stairs.

Siobhan ran past, not with them, tears pouring down her face.

Don't let anyone see! Don't let anyone see!

Her back disappeared into the street . . .

Got to get out!

She followed slowly down the stairs holding the brass rail, feeling her way. Her lynch pin gone, she could trip and fall the complete flight in full view of everyone. That would never do. She called him. Some people turned around and her face felt hot and flushed. He did not hear, or if he did, he kept straight on.

God, she would kill him ! And her!

Outside, on the street, Siobhan was breathing heavily. Tears of shame spilled from her eyes, despite her efforts to stop them. Later as the three walked home together in silence, each nursing their own grievance, she began thinking how much it was costing them to keep their daughter at that school. They had saved and saved to keep up with all the demands. How much were they paying for her to learn to pity them?

Memento Mori

Rose used to have a boxer dog. A large brown creature with a square head, bow legs and a pigeon chest. It had been the runt of its litter which is why Rose ended up with it. She was always a soft touch where animals were concerned.

'I can't bear to see anything suffer,' she told her husband whenever she carried in another stray cat, preferably when it had been run down by a bus or was similarly afflicted.

'I only wish you'd show the same concern for me,' he said with regularity.

'You're not in dire straits like these are,' came the timed response and Eric, always on cue, said that he would have to die first before he got any sympathy.

'If I took ill you wouldn't have time to notice with all the strays you keep bringing back with you. One more and it will be me that leaves home!'

But Rose kept bringing dogs, cats, tortoises, in fact, anything the neighbours wanted rid of, Rose always obliged and he continued to say 'one more, and it will be me that leaves.'

When Rex was about twelve he died. Rose came down in the morning to find him stretched out on the sofa.

'Come on boy!' she called, patting her thigh. Getting no response, she took his lead from the hall stand. He really was sleeping heavily she thought. It must be because he was getting so old. She slipped her hand under his collar to attach the chain and as her fingers touched cold inert hide, her eyes widened. There was no other movement. With a sickening realisation Rose ran upstairs to wake her husband.

'Eric!' she called as she reached the top. 'Eric!'

She flung the door open but there was no reply. He was sleeping heavily, grey hairs beginning to crowd out the dark falling against the stark white of the pillow where his head lay. His mouth hung loosely open in an attitude of disrespect. She went to shake him but stopped midway. Her hand drew back without touching him in a horrid flash of *déjà vu*.

Later that day Eric transferred the dog into the parlour, carrying the animal across his arms and shutting the door on it. Back in the kitchen he wiped his forehead and ran hot water over his hands.

'Trust him to die when the bloody binmen are on strike,' he said, vigorously soaping himself. The entire cleansing department were on a stoppage following an overtime dispute. 'Unsociable hours, unsociable labour and an unsociable workforce' ran the waggish headlines in the local paper and although the strike was in its early satage, no one had any great confidence that it would be resolved quickly, at least not before the rubbish was piling up in the streets.

'Wait until next weekend with the sodding flies round here and that thing in the parlour.'

'You've no respect,' Rose sobbed.

'Respect!' he shouted snatching at the roller towel. 'Good God! I'd have had to slip the binmen a fiver at least to take it away, but God knows what we're going to do now! We can't dig a hole in the park for him you know, its a health hazard,' he added sardonically. 'I'll have to take him down to the knackers yard.'

In the gloomy kitchen Rose's face alone stood out, for it had turned ashen. Across her mind the awful vision of her husband had passed gleefully rubbing his hands as Rex was ground into bone meal. Dancing a strange festive rite in a circle around the public incinerator, cackling like one of the Macbeth witches.

'He was such a noble dog,' she sniffed, beginning to cry into her handkerchief.

'Oh bloody hell! I can see us ending up with a funeral cortege and wreaths. Well don't expect the neighbours to draw their curtains. If you ask me, there will be a lot happier faces round here once they know that that thing is dead. I honestly don't know why we didn't get more complaints than we did, the way it used to bark and howl. It must have kept people awake at night.'

'You never liked him! You never did! You were mean to him . . . ' she clasped the handkerchief tightly to her mouth.

'Look Rose, I don't care how he goes. If you want to hire the

Welsh Guard to beat time as he's carried out, that's up to you. But we have got to get shot of it. I'll take him tomorrow.'

Rose lifted her face and fixed him with a watery stare.

'Over my dead body!' she said.

For two days Rex leant against the piano.

'Don't you touch him!' Rose said whenever Eric went towards the parlour door. 'I'll do it.'

And each evening when he came home from work Eric asked 'Well? Has it gone yet?' Seeing Rose shake her head he would repeat his warning. 'If it hasn't gone by Thursday, so help me I'll lift it out myself and set fire to it.'

Rose did not know what to do.

After five days she phoned the police.

In Granby Street police station the desk officer picked up the telephone wearily. It was nearly the end of his shift, he had been on duty since nine the previous evening.

'You want to report a dead dog?' he repeated slowly chewing on his pencil. 'When did you see it and which street was it on?'

There was a pause while he tapped the pencil's end rhythmically on the note pad in front of him . . . 'O CAN YOU WASH YOUR FATHERS SHIRT O CAN YOU WASH IT CLEAN . . .'

'I'm not sure that I understand . . . you found a dead dog on your sofa when you came down for breakfast. Did you notice anything else unusual?'

With his right hand he drew out a grid and began to fill it in with noughts and then crosses. He only had three quarters of an hour left to do before going home. Bacon and eggs, he thought, being a man of direct if rather basic thought. Maybe a sausage? Yes, why not. He wondered if there were any beans. Just a small tin from the pantry. He wouldn't open a large one just for himself. And a bit of fried bread with some black pudding. If there was any left that was. He could pick up some from the butchers on his way home. MacCawley's made their own on the premises. He began to salivate imagining it hanging up in loops in the window.

'Pardon? Yes I do know that the binmen are on strike but it's good of you to remind me.' He realised with a jolt the matter he was attending to. 'You don't think they had anything to do with it do you?' he asked. 'Ah, yes, I think I see. It's leaning against the piano. What do you mean your husband carried it? But you should never disturb evidence.'

He began to write laboriously: 'Dog found leaning on piano.'

He went back and altered it so it read 'Dog found dead, leaning on piano.' Then he drew a line through 'dead' and moved it to the start of the sentence. There was something decidedly funny going on.

'Are you sure you're telling me everything?' he asked, wanting to follow the correct procedure for gleaning information. He tried to recall the policy. 'Normally we don't deal with dead dogs,' he said in his official voice, 'not unless they're causing an obstruction. Say you found one blocking the road, then we'd remove it or . . . ' he tried to remember the other cause, or if they are a risk to public health. Now, would you consider this dog to be a risk — threatening, or otherwise, to the environment?'

Rose thought for a second. Mrs Furlong's dog had been a risk, they had had to have it muzzled and she had to pay 30 shillings to the police station as a fine. What on earth would they charge her for Rex? She had an irrational fear of the police force. Anyone in a uniform symbolised authority to Rose, even the usherettes in the Rialto creeping up with their red torches made Rose feel guilty. She broke out in a sweat. She didn't want them coming round for the dog and her being dragged out into the street as the owner of something that threatened the community, upbraided for being irresponsible.

'It's all right officer,' she heard herself saying. 'It's gone,' and she slammed the phone down.

Rose was overfond of animals she knew. They were her weakness. Animals and babies. And now that their only daughter had left she felt all the more need to fill their home with young living things, even if it did mean that eventually they grew old and died on her. She wished she had had more than one child, it was her deepest regret. If she could go back . . . but then, that was impossible and what was the point of thinking about it?

Eric was 17 years older than her. He had been a widower when she had first met him. Everyone had frowned upon them then, but she didn't care. He had been good to her and if their union had not been so fruitful as they both might have wished, it was her only regret and she considered herself lucky. Eric had always been fearfully proud of Rose and he delighted in the way she was always well turned out.

'I don't know,' he always said, 'you see some women walking around with curlers in and carpet slippers as if they can't be bothered with themselves. It's a shame that they should feel so insignificant.'

Rose had always been flattered by his obvious pride in her and she did care for his opinion, so that morning, dressed in her neatly pressed black suit for the occasion, she unlocked the parlour door.

There was a slight smell but then the room was musty anyway because it was so seldom used and never heated. In the fireplace stood a bowl of greying plastic tulips with a fan of pleated paper in front of it. The room had the cold look of rooms that were only ever used for laying out the dead, or storing unwanted furniture. Her sewing machine was packed to one side, a sturdy black treadle from the secondhand shop that she had given 15 shillings for. Although still in working order it was impossible to get at. The cast iron base had tins of paint and boxes of tools piled up on it. Even the piano was loaded up with debris: coffee jars full of nails, buttons, and old bits of rusted metal implements gave it the appearance of a counter in a do-it-yourself shop. It was not a room to sit in, or stand in too long for that matter. Rose hated it.

She lifted the stiffening Rex and straining a little, for he was a large dog, managed to lock the door behind them. She found that the best way to carry the dog was under her right arm with her left hand clasped around its underbelly. And this was how she got to the end of the street, half dragging, half lifting him.

It was a hot day and she was perspiring before she reached Princess Boulevard. She noticed a few people looking at her but, as she did not want to stop and explain, she walked past as steadily as she could manage. At the bus stop she put him down. His paws clicked against the white pavement and his shadow cast a lean dark stain behind him. He stood upright, supported entirely by rigor mortis. Behind them a queue began to form. As the first bus approached, Rose wanting to do the right thing stepped towards the platform.

'Excuse me,' she addressed herself to the conductor, 'but is it all right, to bring a dog on the bus?'

' 'Course girl. As long as he behaves himself. Can't have dogs running up and down the . . . ' His jaw dropped open as Rose heaved the rigid Rex up onto the platform. 'He's not too well,' he managed to say. 'There's something wrong with him.'

Rose was trying to fit him into place under the stairs usually reserved for bags and blocking the entrance by so doing. Behind her the queue was growing restless.

'Come on Missus . . . ' Each one stopped as they got a proper look at the dog.

'You'll have to take him off,' the conductor said, while an elderly woman at the front of the bus began screaming.

'Rabies!' she yelled. 'The dog's stricken.' She pointed her walking stick towards the luggage compartment for emphasis.

'That's what they look like. I've seen it before, that look in their eyes.'

'Hey Missus! Has yer dog got rabies?' said a young man behind Rose as he nimbly jumped back down from the platform.

'No, of course he hasn't,' Rose calmly explained with a smile. 'He's dead.'

'Dead!' squealed the old woman. 'The rabies has killed him!'

'Don't be soft mother,' a middle-aged woman sitting next to her said.

'For God's sake get it off,' someone requested.

'Is it contagious?'

'What? A dead dog?'

'Look Missus, you'll have to remove him. I can't have it frightening the passengers,' and the conductor began to tug at the dog which had already become firmly wedged in the space.

He gave one desperate heave and the animal came free. Rose found herself swiftly escorted with her burden onto the pavement where she tottered, trying to regain her equilibrium, while holding Rex upright with his front paws on her shoulders like a partner at the Grafton Ballroom. His back legs began slipping away at the same time that Rose dropped her handbag. She foolishly bent down to try and retrieve it and the dog collapsed.

The bus driver, wondering what the delay was, glanced into his wing mirror in time to see a large dog slide on top of a woman and pin her to the ground.

'Good God!' he exclaimed inwardly, making a move to leave the cab and go to her assistance. But his attention was taken up with the sound of his mate banging against the glass. He wound up the leather blind and saw that the passengers were all out of their seats.

'Drive on for Christ's sake!' his mate mouthed to him, still banging on the glass in a state of extreme agitation.

'But that dog . . . ' he shouted back, pointing to the street where Rose was lying.

'Never mind the bloody dog, I've just put it off the bus.'

'Is it vicious?' he breathed on the window.

'Vicious!' his friend repeated, looking shocked, 'vicious! It's lethal that's what it is. Drive on. Drive on!'

Behind the conductor he could see the gaggle of passengers, all talking at once and moving freely about in the aisle. Through the window he heard muffled words . . . 'Rabid', 'Dead', 'Mother of God, forgive us our trespasses . . . ' for quite a few of them had started praying. 'It's mad, mad.'

Not sure who was afflicted he put his foot down hard on the accelerator.

The sergeant tapped his pencil on his notebook.

'Are you sure you saw the dog attack the woman?' he asked the bus driver. 'Why did you not go to her assistance?'

'It was ferocious man and I had a busload of passengers.'

'If it's true . . . and I'm not saying that I don't believe you,' he added quickly, 'it's just, well . . . a rabid dog is a rare thing in England if that's what it was and I doubt very much . . . '

'I didn't say it was rabid, only mad and dangerous . . . and it's still . . . out . . . there . . . ' The driver pointed a shaking hand to somewhere outside the door, his eyes popping from his head in wide-eyed terror.

'Have you got any witnesses?'

'Come outside mate.'

The sergeant followed him out into the station forecourt where, blocking off the entrance to the parking ground, as well as half of the pavement, was a green double-decker bus.

On Princess Boulevard, Rose was flagging down taxis. She had not had much luck. The first car to stop had driven off again immediately after the driver noticed, over Rose's shoulder, Rex fall sideways and lie rigid on the ground.

'Gerraway!' he said. 'I'm not taking that!'

The reaction of most of the cabs which stopped was similar if not always as vocal. The majority slowed down only to gather speed again without exchanging more than a horrified look.

'I'll pay Sunday rates,' she had offered one car in desperation, to be told that there were other passengers to consider.

'I can't let someone sit down where a minute before there's been a dead dog now can I?' one asked and Rose could not argue.

She stuck her thumb out in desperation at cars. She lugged the dog over to the traffic island at the end of the Boulevard. For if she stood on it she thought that she would have the chance of cars in both directions. She left Rex in the middle, lying on his side, while she ran back and forth from either end of the roundabout hailing passing vehicles. After half an hour she was exhausted. She leant against the pole of a traffic sign and drew her hand across her eyes wondering why life was so difficult. That moment she heard something pull into the lay-by at the park gates. Spinning round she saw that a lorry had stopped and two young people were clambering out from the passenger seat.

'Thanks Mate!' a lanky youth shouted up to the driver who was hidden from view as he helped a fair-haired girl down beside him. Two rucksacks were thrown from the great height of the cab and a voice shouted instructions for how to find the town centre.

Seizing her opportunity and her dog, Rose ran over the road.

'Excuse me, are you going in the direction of the city dump?' she shouted up. 'Or out past Walton?'

'Ay, all right,' said the voice. 'I'm turning off before that, but jump up, I'll take ye as far as Walton Hospital. Any good?'

Rose almost screamed with relief, but controlling herself began to explain. After all, she thought it was only fair to warn him.

'Look,' she began, 'I've got a dog.'

'Och that's all right, I like animals.'

'No, it's . . . you see . . . he's . . . ' she stumbled over the words, her eyes beginning to fill with tears. 'I've had such a terrible time,' she sobbed. 'I . . . I . . . ' words choked her, she began to cry. The driver's head appeared through the window. Peering down he saw Rose for the first time, standing weeping in her smart black suit and he thought there was something odd.

'Are you all right dear?' he asked, wondering whether to pull away.

'My dog's dead!' Rose burst out.

In a flash he was down on the pavement helping Rose up. He lifted Rex up and placed him gently beside her on the seat.

'Isn't it bloody awful,' he said indicating the dog, 'that anyone should be kept waiting that long.'

Eric came off his shift at eleven that morning. He took his time walking from where the factory bus dropped him off to his door, jangling his keys in his left hand. His right hand was free, for he carried no lunch box on Thursdays as he was home for his meal, which on any other Thursday he looked forward to and would hurry along. But today he strolled. He left his tools behind in his locker in the wash-up room, so he was empty handed. Like most nervous people who have difficulty placing their hands comfortably as they walk, Eric today showed his disquiet by the way he rattled his keys for something to do.

Outside the house he hesitated before mounting the step. Today, he thought, he would have to call his own bluff. Poor Rose. He knew that she was upset over Rex, but he also knew that the dog had to be got rid of.

In the hall he called out 'I'm home!' as he hung his donkey-jacket up on the peg. From the living room came the screeches from the cage as the two budgerigars fought over a piece of millet.

'Where's yer wellies?' one of them asked repeatedly.

'Rose?' he called into the empty kitchen. The cat was scratching against the door. He went through and drew back the bolt, opening it a crack letting the sun from the back yard light up the dark flagstones on the floor.

'Come on then Snowy,' he said as a black cat walked knowingly into the kitchen and went straight to a dish on the floor.

'Who the hell are you?' he asked it, looking out into the yard for the other one. It began eating from the plate, and he laughed. 'So, you've come to Doctor Barnado's too have you?' and he rubbed its ears.

'Rose!' he called again. She must be at the shops still, he thought. Then an idea struck him. If he hurried he could have the dog out and away before Rose was back. That would spare her some of the suffering. Yes, if he could act quickly now, he could just tell her that Rex was gone and maybe she would not have to see anything. He ran out to the phone box and dialled the police.

As the panda car cruised along Princess Park the car intercom began to crackle.

'Can you investigate a dog?' the message came through.

'Not another one!' the co-driver exclaimed, taking up the mouthpiece. 'But we've been everywhere looking for this mad one already. Hey! you don't think that it's the same dog do you?'

'Hardly,' the robotised voice answered. 'This one's dead. Bit of a problem disposing of the remains. If you could get round there and check it, then contact the salvage if you think it's necessary and get the bloke to fill in a form O.K.?'

'Will do.'

Rose meanwhile had been let down with her cargo outside Walton Hospital where she struck lucky with a mini-cab driver who was coming away from the visitors' entrance intending to return to his depot.

'The sights I've seen girl,' he said indicating the hospital. 'When you've worked this stretch you get used to all sorts. Come on, let's try and get him in.'

Rose and the man strained and pushed but Rex on account of his inflexible nature could not be coaxed into the back seat.

'Only solution,' he said looking at her, 'is to break his legs.' Noticing Rose's horrified look he added quickly, 'It's all right girl, he can't feel anything. Now hold him steady.' So saying he jumped on his front legs with the full weight of his foot as if breaking wood for a bonfire.

Rex was slid inside through the open windows, where he lay with his front paws projecting from one side, his hind through the other. The only way that Rose could manage to hold him, so that he did not fall out, was to slide in underneath the dog and sit with it laying across her chest.

Poor Rex, she thought gazing up at him as he stared out the window. Tears began to prick at her eyes as the driver took off in the direction of the city dump.

The young constable waited in the hall as Eric gingerly unlocked the parlour door.

'Right,' he said authoritatively stepping in front of Eric into the room. 'Where is it?'

Eric followed behind and looked around stupefied.

'It's not here,' he said sniffing the air cautiously. 'It's gone!'

The constable sighed and drew out his notebook.

'Is it a case of theft you want to report now?' he asked.

From the other side of the city Rose was making her way home by bus. She would probably be a little late with Eric's dinner. She wondered if he might like to go on a picnic instead? They could go to Princess Park and walk around Rex's old haunts. Her eyes suddenly felt warm and she knew that she would cry if she did not sit up and take control of herself quickly. She tried to console

herself. After all, she thought, she had managed to see him off
herself — and it had been a memorable end.

The Application Form

'It's arrived, it's arrived! Wake up you lazy sod!'

Nell pounded her sleeping son, reaching across him as he lay in bed to draw the thin curtains and let more of the bright morning sun flood into his untidy room. A pair of red eyes that were still heavy with sleep stared out from under the blankets hating her. As they gradually focused, their attention was directed not at her but at the brown envelope being waved in front of them. Sleepily Brendan took it from her and put it down on the table. He threw back the covers and got slowly to his feet, looking unsteady and vaguely stupid in his striped pyjamas.

'Well go on! Open it!'

'Oh God . . . in a minute,' he answered dully, stumbling out of the room towards the lavatory. 'Christ!' he blasphemed as he drew the catch.

Nell's face piqued. She had annoyed him with her enthusiasm and now she felt as if she had acted improperly as she waited lamely for him to come back. He felt rotten, but his mother should have learnt that he was always irritable in the morning, she should have known better than to expect anything other from him, he always woke up badly.

Back in his room he attempted a grin, but it was more of a grimace than anything else. His mouth tasted stale and he wished that she would go instead of standing awkwardly by the side of the bed, reminding him with her dejected figure that he had taken the edge off her happiness.

The letter was a formality, for when Brendan's results had arrived they had known that he would be going to Queen's. And there it was, the definite confirmation of his place. All that day Nell walked about in a daze. Her son, going to University! No one in her family had ever done that before. She phoned her sisters and, wanting to tell yet more people, made an unnecessary trip to the shops to drop into the conversation with her best English telephone voice;

'Of course, Brendan's going to the University this Autumn yooneow,' drawing out the words to make the sentence last as long as possible. 'The' University, because Nell thought there was only one.

'What's he going to do there?' Mrs Carmichael asked with a look of disgust. She had either misheard or believed that university was a type of borstal.

Nell thought for a moment. What would he do? More school-work? She had never thought to ask him and she did not have the vaguest idea how the university functioned. She felt rather foolish as she mumbled that he would 'learn things'. It suddenly sounded rather pointless.

'But like what?' Mrs Carmichael asked. 'I mean . . . what sort of things? Hasn't he learnt enough already?'

Nell could see that she was not going to be fobbed off so easily. Sod her, she cursed inwardly. Why did someone always have to be so damned bloody clever?

'Oh they learn all sorts of things nowadays, you know, yooneow . . . ' She was struggling and the other woman knew it.

'No I don't. I can't imagine why anyone has to stay on at school all the time they do now. I was out working when I was fourteen, I'd learnt all they had to teach me by then, me studying was over. What they're filling their heads up with now I can't guess. Sitting at desks like big kids when they could be out earning money.'

'Oh, but they don't look at it like that, they just go on learning. You can never get enough education it seems. When you've learned one thing there's always something else waiting to be studied.'

'Like what?'

God, but she was being awkward this morning. Nell could have kicked her but didn't want to give her the satisfaction of seeing her riled.

'Woodwork, philosophy, architecture, Russian . . .'

'Russian! What's the bloody good of learning that unless he's going to spy.'

Some of the other neighbours started to laugh.

'Is it like a school then this university?' one of them asked.

'I don't really know,' Nell admitted in a voice which was only a little flatter than usual. 'I expect it is. He'll have to read a lot I suppose.'

'Well I think it's wonderful, just wonderful,' Mr Maguire said, nodding with approval. 'And I think we can all be grateful that a fine young man like Brendan is prepared to sacrifice his life to help others.'

Nell stared at him queerly.

'Tell me,' he said turning to her. 'When he comes out does he go straight into the priesthood, or do they send him away to the missions for further training? I mean, is he fully qualified, or does he have to do a bit of practical work first?'

'Och Maguire, you've got it wrong again,' Mrs Carmichael growled. 'He's going to university, not a bloody seminary.'

'Well, well,' Mr Maguire said, not one to be easily dismayed. 'I always said he'd turn out well.'

'But what will he do when he finishes?' old Mrs Daly asked.

'That's a point' . . . ' said Mrs Carmichael turning to Nell. 'What will he do love, you know, when he's finished?'

'He'll get a good job.'

Nell never doubted that this education Brendan was about to receive would fail to unlock the door to a successful life ever after. But the neighbours looked uneasily at each other.

'How long does it take then?'

'Three years, or more if he decides to go on even further.'

They drew in their breath. 'God, but that's a long time. Better get his name down for the Post Office.'

Eileen was genuinely pleased for her brother when she heard the news. She felt saddened too, because it meant that he would be leaving home, and she would miss him. They had always been good friends, always been close. She was also a bit scared by the prospect because she knew what it would mean. Brendan would not live with them again as part of the family. He would only ever return as a visitor from the moment he left to embark on his university career. He would no longer be tied by his father's dominance and stubborn authority. He would be free of it, and Eileen knew that fact alone would change Brendan. He would not be the brother she needed in adversity.

Still, she found consolation thinking that it would only be a matter of two years before she could expect to do the same. If it was possible. Her father had already threatened to bring her out of school when she finished her 'O' levels, but he had not carried out his threat. She was going back that September to the sixth form. But she knew that he was not above changing his mind and so the prospect hung over her like a dark cloud. But she had worked out a solution, if it became necessary. She would leave home at eighteen anyway. There was nothing he could do about that. She would pack a bag and get out. He could not stop her. But she was worried by the next two years without Brendan to back her up. She felt indebted to her brother, because just having someone older than her meant that she had extra time to work things out. She was legatee to Brendan's problems.

When Brendan began to question their faith at the age of sixteen, Eileen was there to experience those doubts with him. By the time she reached that age herself she had already had two years to sort out the same problems. It was as if being two years younger enabled her to develop a better understanding when she reached that same age. It was, she was sure, the only single advantage that she had over him. She was always the more decisive of the two, clearer in her ideas than he was. All their relatives commented on it, that she seemed to understand things. She did. She understood that to her parents Brendan was really the only one that mattered. Her understanding did not spare her any pain, but increased it.

When Brendan spoke her parents listened, especially her mother. Sometimes it almost drove her mad to see her being weighed down by Brendan's adolescent authority. But she could not blame her brother for that. It saddened her to think that he might go through life believing in this power vested from God that all men possessed. He might end up like their father.

'I give the orders in this house!' their father would yell and his wife would nod meekly and agree standing behind her husband, only right and fitting.

Eileen had spotted the warning signs, for Brendan was beginning to show that annoying arrogance he had first displayed at fourteen when Eileen had hated him. He came home from the Irish Christian Brothers' School one day saying, 'What have women ever done? Our physics teacher said women were just the tools of men and that it is our Christian duty not to take advantage of their natural inferiority, because He has made it like that for a purpose. Tools,' he repeated staring dreamily out of the window.

Eileen had felt destroyed. She cried in bed not wanting to be merely a tool. It was so unfair, she could not even be an altar boy. And now again at eighteen he was lording it over his mother, treating her as though she was an idiot. Eileen hated seeing him behave like that. It drove her crazy.

'Make us a cup of tea,' he'd say and Nell would shoot out into the kitchen or worse still, look up at her and say 'well?' nodding towards the kitchen, because her son had made a request and it was right that the daughter should comply. She knew that if she had sat in a chair giving orders she would be told to get it herself, and called every name imaginable. If it came from Brendan it was authority, but if it came from her it was just cheek. Eileen never budged.

Nell could have clouted her. She wondered what was wrong with the girl lately. Didn't she see that she was worked to death? She had just come in and put the shopping down on the table and had to rush out to make tea. But Eileen never thought of offering, not that one, she'd just sit there and ignore everyone. Then she would get up and make herself a cup of tea, without thinking about anyone else. Bloody selfish that's what she was. The last few days in particular she had been getting on Nell's nerves. Sitting there without saying anything, leaving the room whenever she came in. Jealous, that's what it was. She was jealous of Brendan because Brendan was clever.

As she thought of her son a flush of happiness spread across her face. She sorted in the bag for the chocolate biscuits she'd bought especially. She'd take him one with his tea. She had never understood Eileen. She was temperamental, always had been. Even as a baby she had done the most crying. She had not been as lovable as Brendan. Nell imagined him as he had been, chuckling away, playing with a rattle and felt a gag in her throat thinking how quickly her son had grown up. Here he was about to go to University. She remembered his first day at school. He had held her hand nervously going up the road. But he had not given anyone trouble, settling in behind a desk and starting to play with some coloured counters that he found. He hadn't even seen her leave, so absorbed he was. She had come home and cried. It was funny to think of that. But Eileen now, she wasn't at all like Brendan, not easy. Last night for instance, he had only remarked that there was no sugar in his tea and she had hit the roof. Told him to get up and get it himself and called him all sorts of names.

She had had to intervene.

'For God's sake stop arguing!' she had shouted. She hated rows between the kids. She had enough to put up with from her husband without those two following suit.

'Get the sugar bowl Eileen,' she told the girl and what did she do? She let loose a torrent of abuse at poor Brendan's head *and* half the sugar lumps! They went all over the floor. It was a good job their father wasn't there, he'd have killed them. She had a temper that one. God, life certainly was never boring with her around! Nell found herself grinning despite herself. Really it was something she had long wanted to do herself, chuck something at her husband. But it would have to be something a bit more weighty if it was to make any impression on his thick skull, she thought — the kettle, or the coal bucket. But poor Brendan, it was quite comical really. She went back into the living room smiling.

'This came with the afternoon post,' Brendan said fishing a green application form out of his trouser pocket. 'It's for the grant. I've already been down to the education offices and checked, I should qualify for the maximum.'

'Just as bloody well you do,' Nell said sipping her tea, 'because we couldn't afford to keep you.'

'No. Indeed. That is why I, that is, your son, will get a maximum grant . . . 'Brendan explained with deliberate slowness as if talking to someone with difficulty understanding.

Eileen glared at him. 'Just cut out the comedy smart lad.'

'Oh God, not you again!' Nell said turning to her daughter. 'What's wrong with you now?'

'He knows,' she said sullenly sinking back into her chair.

Brendan continued as if nothing had happened.

'The thing is, father has to fill out some bits, but it's straight-forward enough. The sooner he does it, the sooner I'll know for sure what I have to live on next year.'

His mother nodded. She did not ask to see the forms. Why should she? To the water, gas and electricity boards she did not exist. Her name never appeared on any official documents. When-ever brown manilla envelopes with little windows cut out in them came through the door she ignored them, for she had learnt that they were not her concern. It was only her husband who was requested to fill in forms, that was just the way it was and she no longer even had curiosity to see them.

'Show them to your father when he gets home tonight. With a bit of luck you could have them ready and back in the office by tomorrow.'

'I've already filled in the bits I can: dates of birth, other dependent children and all that. So all he has to do is the part about income.'

It was straightforward enough, even rather simple. There should not have been any problems.

'I'm not filling that bloody thing in, and that's final!' His father's voice was harsh. He was beginning to yell. His face was obstinate, the chin stubborn and the mouth set. Brendan expected him to stamp his foot.

He knew that look on his father's face too well. Whenever he had to stick his tongue into his cheek as he was doing now it was a sure sign that he was in his fixed position. Putting his tongue in his cheek was a device he used to stop himself spluttering, which was undignified. It was always accompanied by speeded-up breathing, and a flush of irritation as he became more irrational and heated. Brendan knew that there was no point arguing with his father when he had reached that stage, but he thought he might be able to explain the consequences of his father's reaction and in this way alter the course of threatened events.

'But if you don't fill it in, I can't get a grant, and if I can't get a grant I can't go to university,' he explained tiredly. It was a weariness borne of knowledge of his father's intractable nature.

'For God's sake,' Nell said, 'why can't you just fill the thing in. What harm is there?'

'Harm!' he screamed, 'Harm! You expect me to tell everyone what I earn! Some tuppenny-ha'penny office clerk knowing how much I bring home every week? I'm not filling that in and that's an end to it. You're entitled to a grant. They'll have to give it to you.'

'Not unless you fill in the form. They won't take my word for it. Any one could go down there and say that their parents can't support them. They need to know how much you earn in order to make an accurate assessment; unless you are suggesting that you would rather pay for me, that is, that you are able to.' Brendan's voice was mocking.

'Go to Hell!' his father shouted, striking out blindly with his fist and winding his son in the belly. He had started panting, the look he gave his son was of hate. He despised the young buck, daring to suggest that he didn't earn enough. Let him try to earn his own living. Let's see who does the best at it.

'Go and work in bloody Ford's,' he spat.

Brendan sank back, tears beginning to well up. Don't cry in front of him. Don't let him see that you're upset. Weak, a weakling, mummy's boy. Insults smarted in his head. So that was it, his father's plan for him. Work in Fords. Don't dare dream of getting away from that. It was good enough for him so it must be good enough for the son.

'Bullies are cowards,' his mother always told him whenever he got into trouble at school. 'Stand up to them and they go away.'

But this time it was not so simple. Brendan was powerless while his father triumphed in the display of his control over the boy's life.

He remembered the first time that he had stood up to his father's temper. It was just a little over a year ago. Eileen was not quite fifteen. She was skinny and her hair was still in plaits then. He did not mind him knocking him about, but he could not bear to see him hitting Eileen. It wasn't fair. Even if repetition meant that it had become commonplace and to some extent the girl was used to it, it still didn't seem right to Brendan. He remembered the look of horror and surprise on her face when he had stood between her and their father. Behind him he was still striking out with blows. It took him a while to register that it was no longer his daughter but Brendan's back that the fists were striking.

'The little slut! The little bitch! Lady bloody muck!'

All Brendan had wanted to do was cover his sister's ears so that she would not hear any more insults. That was all he really intended. But once between them, he had swung round and landed a punch squarely in his father's mouth. He couldn't remember who had been the most surprised. But it was the quickest solution to stop him shouting. Thank God their mother had not been there. Nothing was ever said about it after. Their father pretended that it had not happened. But Brendan saw how he was less quick to hit Eileen after that.

He looked over now and saw his sister. She looked terrifying. She was white, completely white, the colour had drained out of her while she had listened to her father telling Brendan that he was still the one who gave the orders. Her father's temper stirred the hatred in the girl. Right then she hated him with every inch of her wiry frame. She wanted to throw herself at him, beat him to blood pulp with her own small fists. Beat and beat until the life went out of him. She despised him for dredging up such violence from her when it should have lain deep and forgotten. Eileen was terrified by her emotions. She knew that at times like this she had anger enough to kill and she retched, disgusted with herself.

Nell was crying. Why did they always have to be arguing. Why couldn't they be like other families? All she wanted was some peace. A quiet life. Hadn't she worked hard all her life and got nothing easy? Hadn't she earned some rest? And this morning she had been so proud, proud enough for the whole street. She had felt as if she would burst until she told everyone her news. And now her husband had destroyed that feeling.

The pen lay on the table, the green application form next to it. All he had to do was to pick it up and sign it. If it was up to her, she would sign it. What possible difference could it make? She remembered the means test as a child. The men in grey overcoats standing in their kitchen. Looking at everything, assessing, making values, telling her mother what she ought to sell. Nell couldn't understand what right they had to come into their home, but she was only a child then. How was it possible? These strangers came and put a price on everything. Her mother's head had hung down, sobbing.

'You've still got a table!' they told her roughly.

They went authoritatively into rooms opening cupboards, investigating.

'What are they looking for Mam?' she asked.

'Hush. Nothing, nothing. I'm a woman on my own. I've no man now,' was all her mother ever said.

'Sell those ornaments,' they commanded. There was no room for attachments, or sentiment. They were poor now.

'Those rings on your finger, are they gold?'

'Please, please, Dear God,' Nell prayed, 'grant my son the chance I never had, Mother Mary I beg of you.' She looked at the pen, it lay resolutely on the table.

Eileen was trying to catch her mother's attention. She waved her arms noiselessly from the kitchen door.

What in God's name is wrong with the girl, she thought. Fancy choosing now of all times to make them all tea! But over the hiss of the boiling kettle Eileen whispered conspiratorially

'Why don't you fill it in — tomorrow, when he's at work?' She nodded in her father's direction. On the other side of the wall the image of her husband burned in Nell's eyes.

'Oh God no, I can't,' she whispered.

'Why not?' the daughter persisted. 'I'll forge his signature! It's simple — they won't bother to check and he need never know.'

'It's not that!' Oh, if only things could be so simple, she thought, suddenly feeling old and tired. 'It's not that at all. But I don't know . . . '

She hesitated, dreading her daughter's clear gaze.

'I mean . . . I don't know what he earns, he's never told me.'

Eileen's mouth opened as if to say something, then closed again. The girl looked stunned.

'Well, a man's got to have his little bit of self-respect,' Nell carried on, but it sounded hollow. She felt irritated. The girl was young yet, she would learn. She would come to see how things had to be a certain way, how things were done.

'Well you know,' she continued, 'It's always been like that.'

Eileen wasn't listening. She was sobbing gently over the tray. Nell was surprised. She felt a sudden overwhelming surge of love for her daughter. Her own eyes began to prick with tears, seeing her own child, the one who was always ready to fight back, to hold her own, now hanging limply, the life gone out of her.

Nell picked up the tray and marched aggressively into the living room. But her courage left her as soon as she saw him. The cups rattled. She put the tray down and it rang like a bell against the polished surface of the table. There was no other sound. Keeping her hand steady she poured him a cup. He took it from her without a word and began to slurp. Christ, he irritated her sometimes! She looked around. Both Brendan and Eileen had disappeared. She felt nervous. She poured herself a cup of tea and raised it shakily to her lips, but she had no taste for it and let it sink back onto the tray before she too left the room.

Something had to be done. Nell couldn't sleep that night — or the next. There was no point arguing with him. The more he was pushed, the more he resisted. She knew him too well. What may have been over-reaction now became solid policy. If he were to give in now, he would look weak, irresolute. So while Brendan had pleaded, desperately, he had furthered no cause other than his father's obstinacy.

That morning he had asked his father if he would consider disowning him legally. He had found out that he wouldn't need the signature if he was 'disinherited'. The word had made Brendan laugh. What did he stand to inherit beyond his father's name? His father's example?

He had sworn at Brendan, called him a bastard anyhow. 'I've got no son! You're no son for me!' He stormed out of the room after striking haphazardly at Brendan's head.

They were at stalemate: he refused to talk and, of course, he would not disown his son publicly. Nell could have told Brendan as much. What a scandal! So while he walked around pretending to have no son, playing a game of silence with him, ignoring him and looking past him and enjoying his own stubborness, his ploy of 'let's see who cracks first!', he would not put his argument on solid ground. It was private. He wasn't going to have some clever-dick lawyer meddling in his business!

Nell lay in the dark listening to him breathing. God how he slept — with a clear conscience. She was tortured. She so desperately wanted her son to go to University. It was so near her grasp to be so cruelly wrenched away — and by her husband! There was no sense, no logic, in what was happening. What should have been a wonderful occasion had been changed to one of misery. Tears ran down her face. Why was he doing this to her? He was blighting his own son's life, nipping the bud before it flowered. When Brendan should have been given every chance to get on in life, she thought, how could he make his way in the world if his own father blocked him? To Nell it was a matter of utmost urgency. One day Brendan would have to support a family. Surely he would stand a better chance if he was educated. Why couldn't her husband see that?

'Jesus, send me guidance,' she implored.

At the first light she rose and blessed herself with holy water from the wall font. 'In the name of the Father and of the Son and of the Holy Ghost, Amen,' she recited mechanically.

She might have been the ghost, she thought ruefully as she caught sight of herself in the dressing-table mirror — the unheard, unseen, performing the sign of the cross. Why couldn't she sign the form? Why did it have to be their father? 'Father! Father! Bloody Father!' she cursed, but an idea began to form. While she knew that she was powerless to make him listen, she did know that there was somebody else, somebody whom she would only have to threaten him with.

The following Saturday she came home with her shopping basket and laid it squarely on the kitchen table in front of him.

'The price of butter's gone up. And cat food! Look at this,' she said piling tins up in a pyramid and pointing to the price labels. 'We'll have to shoot the cat next!'

The ginger tom looked up at her, then put its head between its paws and continued to sleep. The newspaper rustled slightly. From behind it her husband mumbled something.

'I called in on Father Gormley . . .' she continued brightly, hoping her anxiety would not show, 'to ask for advice.'

Had her voice suddenly grown louder? She must try to keep it even.

'I thought that he might be able to help us. About Brendan.'

'What!' He laid his paper to one side and stared at her.

'Well,' she said, trying not to flinch. 'I just thought that he might know a way of getting round those forms. You know . . . I mean . . . maybe he could sign them for us and vouch that we can't afford to keep Brendan at University. They would have to accept the word of a priest, wouldn't they?'

His mouth dropped open.

'I only explained to him how difficult it was . . . I mean, it is, isn't it?'

She tried to sound as if she was in agreement.

'I don't know what you earn, so I can't fill it in.'

'You told the priest that!'

'Well of course. I had to explain the situation. I must say, he did seem rather surprised. He kept saying that he had always found you to be reasonable before . . . funny that, isn't it?' She hoped she sounded guileless. 'I mean, you said yourself that they had no right to ask you such things. I explained that you were refusing on the grounds of privacy . . . ' but she looked acutely embarrassed . . . 'it's nothing to be ashamed of, you said so yourself.'

'I'm ashamed all right!' he yelled. 'I'm ashamed of my bloody wife! That she could be so damned stupid!'

Nell winced as if she had been struck. This was what she was most scared of. She had to remain cool and not shout back, for if she lost her temper she might tell him the truth — that she was too ashamed to speak to anyone about it. She could not have endured the pity from her neighbours, pity for being married to such an oaf. She kept him secret for her own self-respect.

'Anyway, Father Gormley said that he would come round to have quiet word with you . . . he'll probably sign the forms then.' She tried to sound as if she really believed it.

'You stupid cow! By Christ. I'll kill you!' His face was pink.

'Whatever is wrong?'

'Do you always go blabbing to the bloody priest, letting him know all our business? What are you, a total moron?'

Nell looked at him straight. 'I always tell the priest . . . everything.'

He had never struck her, he thought. She ought to be grateful. He thought he was a model husband because he did not beat his wife. The kids . . . well, that was called discipline. God, he didn't want to see the priest now!

'Get me those forms!' he ordered. He would sign the things and have done with it. 'And you can tell the priest it was a false alarm!'

He'd fix it, he thought. Tell him his silly wife had made a mistake — ha, ha, you know Father, ha ha, women . . . That would do it.

Upstairs Eileen was jumping and hugging her brother who held the green form ready to go into an envelope. His future was sealed.

'Come and live with me when you're 18,' he had said. 'Then you will be a legal entity. Dad won't be able to mess you around.'

Brendan knew that she would have a harder time of it. He put his arms round her wanting to offer support. She felt steel-framed and angular. He felt her hesitate a moment, as if she would push him away. His sister needed no one. He had always been a little in awe of her resolve. She had an ability to go out and get things done on her own. She did not need the approval of others that he so desperately sought. Now he needed her. He wanted to know that he could help her and that she would not reject him. Eileen did not blame her brother. 'You'll face this in two years. Only mam won't support you like she has me you know.'

She knew. She had long ago learnt it. She softened and they both cried into each others shoulders as they had done years ago when they were small and used to fight and stop to make friends, each sobbing with fear that the other would not want to.

Downstairs their mother was giving thanks in front of the statue of Our Lady.

'In the name of the Father and of the Son,' she began without the slightest trace of irony.

Specimens

'Isn't it funny how you can go off people?' brooded the dark-haired girl drawing her knees up and hugging them. But her eyes were puzzled.

'Only last week I was wild about him,' she said, talking mainly to herself. 'Imagine! I was lying awake at nights, while now . . .' but as the words evaded her, her mouth turned down in a look of disgust, more expressive than any phrase she could have spoken. Even she was surprised, this time, by the suddenness in her change of feelings.

'I despise myself when I'm like that,' she admonished herself fiercely. 'I go out of control — I'm not able to see straight,' she almost spat in self-hate.

'Ah, love is blind,' quoted Fiona as she stretched her legs. Molly's face relaxed into a grin.

Both girls were strikingly alike. They both shared the same dark colouring, the same course-textured brown hair that verged on black and grew thick and unruly far down below the hairline of the neck; the same clearness of complexion with its flush of high pink spread over the cheekbones. But it was a clear blue of their eyes which marked them out. It was as if their eyes had somehow been set in the wrong faces. Pale and iced, as if with a light that had its origins in the snowy reflections of chilled landscapes.

They were as similar as sisters and were often mistaken for them, although there was no family bond and sisterhood was a particular impossibility as they had only four months difference in age between them.

Fiona was always mistaken for the eldest.

'It's because I'm tall,' she explained. But height was not the main factor that gave rise to this assumption. She did appear older but it was due to her having a more sober temperament than

164

Molly. She had a reticence which did not come from shyness and was uncommon for her years. It was this alone which confused people and threw them off her scent.

'Ach, he wasn't that bad,' she replied to Molly's extreme. 'But I always knew that about him — didn't you?'

'Well me mam never liked him, she said that he parted his hair on the wrong side of his head and his eyes were too deep-sunk. She said she was always uncomfortable with him. It was as if he was going to pull out a notebook and start taking down particulars. He reminded her of a store detective!'

Fiona guffawed, rolling onto her back and rocking from side to side on the bed.

'But I understand what she means,' Molly laughed, as Fiona tried to right herself. Her eyes had fixed on a point in the middle distance and were staring glassily, mesmerised by the sound of her own voice.

'He was never a friend though,' she continued and her face at once was puzzled, stumbling across another of life's mysteries. 'Not like you and me. We were never really able to talk, not like this. Mam didn't like leaving us on our own.'

She rolled her eyes at the stupidity of mothers. If her father had still been alive he too no doubt would have heaped scorn.

'I think it was harder for us to be . . . friends. Because we "went out" we didn't just "stay in" if that's the opposite. It's harder to talk in a pub or a cinema, oh, you know what I mean!'

'What were his parents like?' asked Fiona matter of factly.

'Dunno, never met them. They live in Essex.'

'Didn't he talk about them?'

'Oh, yeah. He's got three brothers. One's an architect, another's at univeristy doing law. That's what his father did, he's a barrister. The youngest's still at school. He's younger than us. Terry said he's thick and he'll probably end up in teacher training college.'

'Jesus!' blasphemed Fiona. 'Did you tell him what your father used to do?'

'Oh yeah. He knew me dad was a factory worker before the accident. When I first told him he gave me a speech about the conditions of workers under capitalism and how the trade unions were the organs for changing their lot.'

Both were daring the other to be the first to laugh.

'I thought he was great though,' Molly added quickly. 'You

know, the way he was always involved in politics seemed like he really cared about the likes of . . . ' she stopped herself abruptly.

When she spoke again her eyes had narrowed to cold slits.

'But some of those friends of his,' she said reproachfully, 'the ones that were supposed to be comrades. Who kept flying round selling newspapers and talking about this meeting and that meeting in front of me, knowing full well that I couldn't go . . . They were the ones that really irritated me. It was as if I didn't count because I didn't go to their bloody meetings, know all the same crew. I dunno, it was like I wasn't there the way they just ignored me. And when they did talk to me they made me feel so bloody stupid for still being at school. Some of them weren't nine months older than me I'll bet, but every chance they rubbed it in. They were at "university",' she sang in mimicry. 'Christ! You'd think they turned up there fully grown without setting foot in a school first! I think that's why I liked him so much. He said universities were the "last bastions of bourgeois ideology" and they needed to be subverted into centres of education for the workers.'

'Yes. He was different from the others,' said Fiona staring at the pink floral stripes of the wallpaper. She began counting the flower heads. She had to reach 60 before a car went past outside — if she did not something awful might happen.

She counted urgently to avert some future disaster . . . 45, 46, 47 . . . her eyes moved up and down the rows.

'No, that's the trouble,' Molly said. 'Because he wasn't like them I suppose I felt more let down . . . 'Her voice trailed off, remembering.

The first time that she had met Terry was with Fiona. They had gone along to a dance at the student's union. They had both been terrified, not sure whether they could get in.

'We're not students,' Fiona kept repeating to Molly, 'they'll know.' But Molly would not be put off.

They had had to find someone to sign them in.

'Oh let's go home,' Fiona said in despair. 'Look at all those beards, I feel soft.'

But Molly had kept on stopping people as they went past until eventually a couple signed for them. Inside Fiona panicked. When someone casually asked her what she did, in a fit of nervousness she told them she was a secretary and grew pink when she overheard Molly admitting that she was still at school.

'What did you want to tell them that for?' she said. But Molly was proud of being the only member of her family not to leave at fifteen and she also knew that she did not look older than she was, unlike Fiona, who could have passed for 20 when she was made up.

After two halves of lager Molly felt emboldened and when she saw the boy standing at the bar wearing a badge that said 'Troops out of Ireland' she thought he might be Irish and asked him which part he was from.

'I'm from the theoretical wing,' he'd told her and seeing her confusion had apologised and told her Essex.

'Oh,' she said lamely. 'Are yer mam and dad Irish then?' he had laughed at the idea. Something about it amused him greatly.

'No, no they're not. They're both English and as straightlaced Tory as they come,' he spluttered and seeing the look cross her face again, apologised for laughing.

'You don't have to be Irish to support the National Liberation Movement. While six counties are still occupied by the army of British Imperialism the workers in the mainland should support the Irish workers in their struggle for a thirty two county state under workers' control.' And his eyes had glazed as she noticed they often did when he talked politics.

Sometimes he seemed to be reading from one of those things Fiona told her about. Idiot cards she called them. Those things that the Queen used at Christmas, and newscasters read from to speak information that did not touch them. But she had been impressed that someone so English should take another's struggle to heart.

'Me mam's Irish,' she told him. 'And me dad was.'

'Unconditional support for the provisional IRA,' he'd said.

'Christ! Me mam says they're cowboys!'

'Reactionary moralism!' had been his comment.

'58, 59, 60 . . . ' Fiona counted. 'Remember that rotten party we went to with Terry? Where no one did anything all night except stand round like lemons talking about their degree courses. No one said a word to me. Still I expect it's a good job because if they had I couldn't have answered. I hadn't read any of them books they were all talking about.'

'I don't think any of them had. I thought me knees were going to seize up with all that standing around.'

'They don't seem to like dancing do they, that lot?'

'No. They're all too busy preparing to be leaders of the people.'

Terry had been fond of telling them that the working class was formless.

'It needs shape and direction,' he often repeated. 'Without a strong cadre of leaders it will lose its momentum. It needs committed dedicated people who will lead the working class to victory, for without a revolutionary party there can be no working class revolution. The workers must be organised by a clear decisive leadership with a socialist party. Remember that a revolutionary party is the memory of the class. It is the store of working class experience. The majority of workers are uninformed and conservative. The revolutionary leaders and conscious elements will influence and educate that majority.'

Molly could hear his voice, its smooth well modulated tone. It was repetitive in its role of educator, without fire, without spontaneity, lacking his print on it as if it did not belong to him; still, with all those raw uninformed workers for him to influence and lead he must have thought that he had stumbled onto a gold mine last weekend when her mother had the house full with relatives.

The previous Saturday Nell, Molly's mother, had been besieged with visitors. They seldom turned up singly, always bringing their children with them, but this time three different family groups had appeared one after the other.

'Good God!' Nell exclaimed as the door bell rang yet again and Molly shepherded in another uncle and aunt. Nell scurried off into the kitchen to hunt down the porter cake that she had laid up at New Year which was only brought out for 'occasions'. She stood on a chair to reach the tin and passed it down to her sister. As the lid was prised off the aroma of the cold moist cake spread into the air.

'Isn't it just like a wet field,' said Molly's Uncle Thomas, sniffing expectantly and with admiration.

'There's nothing else quite like it Nell,' he acknowledged as he accepted a slice.

Meanwhile the oven had been lit and two small cousins were given the job of scrubbing potatoes and placing them in neat rows on the racks. Molly was despatched to the off-licence by her uncle to buy Guinness and a 'wee drop'.

'Och, sure the girl's 18 now, they'll serve her, but take a shopping basket with you.'

'Ay,' shouted Nell, 'and give next door a knock as you go past.

Tell them to come in. If you see old Michael tell him to bring his mandolin.'

Molly had been taking lessons from him. He was self taught and understood no formal music.

'You feel the sound,' he always said splaying his calloused fingertips for emphasis, 'and you know by the feel whether the note is true.

But Molly couldn't feel any difference. All her family played music by ear except for her. Even Nell, with her raw chapped hands, could pound out a tune on the piano although she played routinely, without a touch for it. But she could not read a note of music whereas Molly could read the notes but had no ear for them. Nell started beating the piano and the eldest boy grabbed the neighbour's grandmother under the armpits and started spinning around the kitchen with her in time to the music.

'Oh God, slow down Mrs Dillon for mercy's sake,' she wheezed, laughing as she was whirled out through the parlour door.

In an instant everyone was up and dancing. Even Uncle Thomas with his rheumatic knee wanted to join in the action. There was a scrabble not to be left out of the fun, a desperation to be in the thick of things. And each one wanted to perform, to contribute in one way or another to the event. The furniture was moved back and Sile gave a bit of step dancing, high and straight with her back like there was a stick down it and her legs lifting high as if they weren't attached to her trunk, no ripple of movement did they cause upwards into her torso. Molly couldn't do that, her back always grew charged with energy and before she knew it her hands and arms were joining in the dance in some variation of her own. But Molly could sing and she knew no awkwardness about singing in public for from early on she had been accustomed to standing in front of an audience and performing. And she had a good repertoire of gaelic songs.

The dancers settled themselves and Molly stood alone. Unaccompanied, her high clear voice reached beyond the small parlour and out into the dark wet street. Her young voice was telling of an Ireland that none of them had known so ancient was its history. When she had finished several of the women and her Uncle Thomas had tears on their faces. No one spoke for a while, scared to break the spell she had cast.

The door bell rang, grating and intrusive. Molly jumped having forgotten that Terry was calling for her.

'Och ask your young man in, love,' her aunt said.

'Aye, we're short of men for the next dance.'

Molly felt awkward as she stood at the door wondering what to do next. She shrunk from bringing him in.

Nell was putting records onto the gramophone. Ceili music reached out into the street. 'The Walls of Limerick.'

Yelps and howls of the dancers. 'Eeeh Hah!' shrieked someone mid twirl. Terry looked puzzled while Molly tried to speak.

'We're looking for partners for the Connaught Reel,' said Molly's Aunt Roséan as she swept past her, 'and here's one fine young man to join in.' She took his arm and propelled him into the parlour.

'Evening Mrs Dillon,' he managed to say as he was taken through and stood at the end of a row.

'Just follow me,' Roséan was winking, 'you don't have to be the greatest dancer in the world to do this one.'

Terry was pulled sideways and forwards in time to the music. He had, after all, been a sport Molly thought. He'd been greatly amused by all the proceedings and kept repeating to Molly how 'this type of thing' wasn't to be found everywhere, until eventually Molly felt odd, uncomfortable, because her family weren't the ubiquitous culture that Terry kept referring to.

Each time he exclaimed 'this is amazing!' Molly winced. He was on the brink of a new discovery and her stomach muscles were contracting. She felt them tighten as he pared down her family to quaint customs and folklore. They weren't people to him but living history. They were specimens that he would have liked to itemise, putting them in formalin for posterity, hanging in timeless blue liquid without sound or movement or life. The leader of the people had at last discovered the leaderless.

She thought that his eyes looked possessive, predatory and she felt the irrational shocking urge to kick him. She watched him as he leaned back against the piano talking to Donal the eldest boy. In his right hand he held a cigarette which bobbed and flowed as he spoke. Molly though that he had beautiful hands, artist's hands. White and long and graceful. They cut and sculpted the air as he spoke, with their dancing expressive way, illustrating a sentence, and now holding a single word for emphasis. They were small, almost too small for a man. Their correct description was 'dainty'. They were a courtesan's hands from Victor Hugo's Paris.

Comfortable, surrounded with silk and lace. In the small front parlour they were out of place. Fish out of water she told herself without taking her eyes away from them. She was fascinated by them. There was something about those hands, something she wanted to know.

Suddenly the right hand arched and shook itself sending a shower of ash floating to the carpet. It lay, a dusty white stain that would be trodden in. It must have been an accident, things always got spilt at parties. But while she watched she saw the hand arch again, slowly, deliberately. It shook itself decadently, sending a second powdering of ash precisely where it was intended. It was cold and calculating. Molly felt herself choking. He must have known that either she or her mother would have to clean it up the next day. The leader of the people was turning them into cleaners, sweeping the path he trod, following it gratefully.

Molly stepped back out of the doorway. She retreated into the kitchen not wanting to look at his eyes, no longer seeing the rest of him.

'But what made you go off him so suddenly?' Fiona's voice called her back. 'Was there anything in particular or was it really his friends that annoyed you? I mean . . . you can't hold him responsible for them can you?'

Molly shrugged. 'Ach, it sounds silly Fiona,' she said, knowing that what she felt would be impossible to put into words. She couldn't even think of how to begin, how to describe what had hurt the most. An unspoken insult that had lain beneath the surface, waiting to spit its venom if it was ever disturbed. Fiona's eyes were quizzical. Molly owed her some sort of explanation.

'It was his hands,' she said lamely. 'I found them disgusting.'

And she was surprised when she looked down to discover that her own had unconsciously curled themselves up into fists.

Aer Lingus

At the ages of 63 and 60 respectively, Nora and Kitty boarded an aeroplane for the first time in their lives and flew to America.

Nora clung to her set of rosary beads and pushed her little sister in before her knowing that it would take all her faith to keep them airborne. During most of the journey she silently mouthed the rosary and hardly dared look out of the window, scared that if she stopped fingering the beads for longer than a few seconds the craft might fall from the sky and drop like a stone into the ocean.

They were both terrified by the hugeness of it all. America was roads going to infinity, fields as far as the eye could see, towns that never ended, the tallest skyscrapers in the world, buildings that disappeared into cloud banks; the biggest, the widest, the greatest.

In their minds' eyes everything looked giant-sized and night-marish. It was a land peopled with shadows, for weren't all immigrants shadows? Immigration blocked out the sun as it stretched back over their family. There was no return from its plunge into darkness. The Irish, and generations of the once Irish, roamed all over the globe rolling soil between their palms and cursing the blight that had packed them like cattle into coffin-ships. Nora and Kitty had been told how their great uncles had sailed to the New World from Ireland. They vanished absolutely, leaving nothing of themselves but holes in the ground where they had torn up clumps of soil to take with them and plant in foreign fields.

'But that's how it was in those days,' they were both fond of repeating.

They would try to imagine the family that they never knew.

When their grandmother arrived in Liverpool (America being too expensive to send daughters), the shackles where the black slaves had been chained still remained along the docks. It was probably the first time that she had been away from home. What must she have felt like, pushing her way through the crowds at the quayside as the most recent wave of cheap Irish labour was shipped into the harbour?

She had been a seamstress, turning hems by hand, putting darts, pleats, tucks and fine feather stitches onto the material she stitched. Her open-work embroidery was admired in the neighbourhood. They still had a white tablecloth at home that was her work, carefully preserved in tissue paper and brought out at Christmas. A lovely delicate thing. In a rare photograph she wore wire-rimmed spectacles and stared out of the print with tired eyes that did not focus on the distance, the keen edge of vision broken down.

She always said sewing the black cloth was the hardest. They remembered her as an old woman, always with a piece of sewing in her lap. Mending and darning for herself with the same skill and deft fingers that had stitched together some fine silk or damask for a customer. She was lucky not to have been forced to mill work. With her constitution she would certainly have developed the bloody cough of consumptive Liverpool. It must have been shocking to her, coming from the country. But here, at least, was survival.

She met and married their grandfather, a Cavan man who had arrived to work the winter. He was the eldest son and had been the last at home, the eldest who inherited a farm and could not make it pay for itself. He had buried his mother and father, and, having nothing else to keep him at home, told the neighbours that he would be back to plough the next season. He put a padlock on the door and never returned. In his absence the walls of the house were not lime-washed, none of the neighbours wanted to take on that job. In the repeated rain the lime wore off and the rough understones were exposed. The mud holding them together dissolved and the house went slowly back into the field from which the raw materials had come. He went back once after 40 years. He knew no one and no one knew him.

Nora grew up by the Mersey with a fear of sea and rough crossings. Sea sickness was an incurable disease as long as the ferry continued to plough nightly between Liverpool and Belfast.

As a child she used to dream about the clank of drawbridges and sirens from the docks. She would cling to the mattress and draw the blankets tight around her, scared lest the bed became a ship in the night and floated out to sea with her on it, leaving her without friend or family, just some addresses on a scrap of paper . . . her lifeline.

Her father, an Ulsterman, had always said that Ireland was a great place to die in, leaving her a picture of Ireland populated with gravestones in green fields. As luck would have it, she married a man from Derry, who, like her father, believed that England was to be a better place to live in. But the dream was false.

The latest wave of emigration took their children to Australia and New Zealand on assisted packages. Kitty's family went out on oilrigs, or to hot places she could not find on the map. Jeannie, her eldest, went to America while Nora's youngest daughter went to London. But it might as well have been America too: Nora had no idea of distance — only that you could not see people every day. Bridget came home for holidays, was always back for Christmas and tried to get up for weekends — but Nora would never have thought of venturing down there herself. Yet here she was, en route to America with Kitty. Her recent widowhood had precipitated Nora's decision to come along with her sister. Kitty had been on her own for years, but Nora was still adjusting to it.

She wondered what Liam would have thought. They had never left the city — only for occasional day trips to North Wales, or Chester. Now here she was, on the brink of the journey of a lifetime: terrified in case she let Kitty down and worried about her aching feet.

'I don't suppose we'll get any younger,' Kitty joked as she stroked back the grey hair that had been carefully rinsed the week before at the hairdressers.

'You know,' she said, seeing Nora's blank look, 'when we go over the dateline . . . four hours, we lose four hours don't we?'

'That won't make much difference to me now Kitty. Four hours isn't much to knock off 63 years.'

'SSHHH!' hissed Kitty. 'Don't let everyone know!'

'Oh, for God's sake, I'm past caring,' and she kicked her shoes off disapprovingly. 'Me bunions are aching again. It's these damn shoes, they have me crippled. I should never go shopping with you, you're an insane influence.'

Kitty started to laugh. 'Oh, well they are awful smart Nora.'

'Och, what's the use in looking smart if I can't walk? It's a waste of money. I should never have been talked into them. I'll have to buy slippers when we get there.'

'Oh Nora! I'm not walking around America with you in daft looking slippers, they'll think I'm your nurse.'

'Well I can't walk in these things.'

'But you can't walk round America in slippers, either.'

'Why ever not? What sort of a country is it that you can't wear slippers in — it's not against the law you know!'

'Look Nora I want to enjoy this holiday. I don't want our relatives feeling sorry for us. I've bought a sun suit.'

'A what?'

'A sun suit. Well it gets hot in California you know,' she said as Nora's eyes widened in horror. Why did she always feel that she had to justify herself to her sister? It got on her nerves.

'What's wrong in wanting to enjoy myself? ' Kitty said angrily. 'I'm going on holiday, not a bloody convalescence.'

'Och, it will be no holiday if they have to carry me everywhere because I'm bloody crippled. Talk sense!'

Kitty stared at the cinema screen, hating her sister. It was the second film she had watched. Nora couldn't stop praying long enough to relax and watch one. Kitty put her headphones on, cutting out her sister completely. 'Talk sense, talk sense,' she sang mockingly in her head. Why did Nora always have to be so sensible? Whenever she wanted a good time, Nora could always be relied on to bring her down to earth, always ready to remind her of how old she was and how old she would be next birthday.

'You're no spring chicken.' That was one of her sister's favourite phrases. Whenever Kitty went to C & A's, Nora always dogged her steps with her calm voice of reason.

'Be careful what you get now Kitty — you don't want to end up looking like mutton dressed as lamb.'

Mutton! If she left it to Nora they would both be dressed in dark sober colours, matching twinsets and smart hats. Only tasteful accessories allowed: a scarf knotted like a cravat, discreet jewellery. Kitty loved pink and purples of all shades and large costume jewellery that she bought on the sly at the bead counter in Woolworths. The bolder the better. Once she read something in a women's magazine about expressing one's personality through dress and she stitched a packet of assorted sequins around the neck of a plain white blouse to jazz it up. All around the binding there were flashing dots of colour, violet, blue, green, yellow, all changing as she moved. She felt it must express something.

'It expresses that you're bloody daft, that's what.' Nora had told her.

Kitty dug her nails deep into her palms and tried to watch the film.

She loved films. Everytime she saw one she was transported and felt that she was the star of it. She loved, best of all, the way everyone was well dressed. The women wore large hats and nobody shouted names at them or stared as they walked along the street. And they had no difficulty walking either, no matter how high the heels on their shoes were. No one in the films ever complained of bunions. She loved musicals best. Nora couldn't stand them.

'I don't know what you see in that,' she said every time there was one on the television. 'Bloody daft that is. Who in the name of God bursts out into song in the middle of Tesco's? Only Minnie Green Hat carries on like that and everyone knows she's three sheets ever since the operation.'

Nora had a way of cutting through all the magic Kitty wanted to spin around herself. She had been the one who had told her that there was no Father Christmas; just like that, the plain truth. Kitty cried as her fragile dream was shattered.

'You had to find out sometime,' Nora had said, scared by her distress. 'Sooner or later you would have found out.'

'You could have waited!' Kitty screamed and ran upstairs sobbing. She had never forgiven her sister that.

And yet she always felt that she was being silly, that she was incompetent, a child who needed guiding into the mature adult world of her sister. Now she wanted to cling on to a younger life while Nora wanted to drag her into the pensioned world of senior-citizen bus passes and concessionary prices at the hairdressers. Kitty was resisting with every ounce of strength, hanging on, screaming, to middle-age.

Kitty felt Nora's prodding and took the headphones off in bad grace.

'What?' she snapped.

Her sister's voice was subdued when she spoke, wanting to effect a conciliation.

'Maybe I could get something flat and comfortable that looks smart. You know, sort of American.'

American. The New World. America. The name sounded new and strange. America! It came out loudly. Nora did not realise that she had shouted as her voice rose in anxiety to yell at the end of the sentence.

America Amer-ica, -ica, ica. Hiccuping nervously Nora wondered how anyone in their family could have gone out there to live. Just going on holiday struck fear into her soul.

'At least they will all speak English. Mrs Reilly went to Lourdes last August, and couldn't even ask for a glass of water. We'll have no problem with the language,' Kitty said trying to quell the fears that were creeping up on her.

'No, no, we won't will we?' mumbled Nora, wanting to feel reassured instead of feeling a nervous choking sensation. She thought that Kitty looked wonderfully calm as she listened to the film. Nora's fingers were twitching, turning the beads over in her cardigan pocket. She settled with one between her thumb and index finger and started saying the Last Decade.

Kitty was using the headphones to block out her sister, but she was not seeing the film. Instead she saw, unfolding in front of her, the way that she had stood tearfully at Speke Airport eleven years ago. Jeannie had tried to reassure her, saying that times had changed, that she was not gone for good, that America was not the end of the world. But Kitty could not be consoled. She felt that she was going to lose her daughter. Jeannie had made light of it, or had tried to.

'I'll be able to save up and come back for a holiday.'

Kitty had not seen her since.

She wondered how eleven years of living in America would have changed her. The time would have made a big enough difference, regardless of anything else. She tried hard to imagine Jeannie. She had the most recent photographs that she had sent over. But it was impossible. She kept coming back to the way she looked when she had first gone out there. She was nineteen, going to be an au-pair for two years. But the two years grew into four and the chance to study. Then there was a teaching post then, later, an assistant in a university department. Jeannie had not been content to stay washing dishes or looking after a rich woman's child. She would not rest until she was in that rich woman's shoes. Every achievement she made put off her life in Liverpool until it became no more than a memory.

Kitty wondered if she would ever come back. Everytime a letter with its postmark thudded to the mat Kitty felt dreadful, reading how well her child was doing. She didn't want her to fail, but she would have preferred her to be home and married to some local boy. And then Jeannie started mentioning one name more than others. Of course Kitty had noticed if she sometimes talked about a boy friend, but this one name kept cropping up and seemed to be special. Eventually Jeannie started writing that she 'hoped they would like each other when they met,' and Kitty panicked. What a mouthful his name was! Enrico De La Montez. That was Rico for short. Now where in the name of God was he from, with a name like that? Detroit she had been told. Kitty could not take it all in. She still hoped that Jeannie might pack a case and return home with them at the end of their holiday.

'I'll bet she's a real Yank,' she said excitedly, growing more fretful by the minute and hoping that she sounded normal.

America was like nothing they had ever seen before.

When Jeannie drove out to meet them she found them in the arrival lounge. They were still clutching the same plastic carrier bags they had left home with that morning, containing uneaten cheese sandwiches and a vacuum flask of tea that they would not travel without. Nora saw Jeannie first and fell to her knees to bless herself with relief that they were not being abandoned at the airport, a fate she had secretly imagined all the way from leaving Speke.

'Praise be to God!' she mouthed, as she dropped to the floor and had to be helped up by Kitty, who had seen nothing and wondered whether her sister was praying or was over-exhausted.

At the sound of the drawling 'Hi, mom!' she spun round to come face to face with the one she had last seen eleven years ago. There was a small silence while mother and daughter looked at the stranger each of them confronted. Jeannie moved her eyes over the entire surface of her mother's face, recognising, re-discovering, finding the stamp of years there. Kitty shook and started to cry, each sob louder and more certain than the last. She covered her face with her hands and wept hysterically while Nora made the sign of the cross.

'Oh God, oh God,' was all Kitty managed to say, 'You never used to have blond hair!'

Jeannie's flat was small, perfectly adequate for one person, but Kitty realised with a shock that Enrico was also living there. He was at the door waiting for them and he welcomed them in like it was his home. It made her feel awkward, seeing them together. This well poised woman was not the daughter she had expected. She had not expected her to live with a man, but Jeannie didn't seem to think that it was at all scandalous, and Kitty knew that she had absolutely no right to criticise. Her daughter's life would carry on after she had returned, so what was the point in disapproving? No one asked her opinion, although she would not have hesitated to give it. She wasn't sure if this was the daughter that had left, if this was the daughter she wanted after all. Nora raved and gushed about the curtains and the carpets and the channels on the television.

'Good here isn't it?' she said, eating doughnuts as if she always had them for breakfast.

Kitty felt as if her heart was breaking. Her daughter's life was so entirely different and she stood there like a stranger in someone's home. An interloper. She was no longer a mother but a long distance relative.

Nora loved it. 'Isn't he nice Kitty? He's a good laugh. A decent sort of a bloke.'

Kitty never passed any sort of a comment one way or the other. He was Italian. His parents were Catholic, that was something in his favour. He was very dark and very different, a foreigner. How, she wondered, could her daughter feel comfortable? She didn't even feel right with her daughter. It wasn't Enrico that was the stranger, it was her.

The photographs were fun. Pulling things out, looking for change, trying to find each other in the lost years before they became unrecognisable.

'Oh I've seen that one. You sent us a copy last Christmas. Your hair was a lot longer then wasn't it?' Kitty said, dwelling on the earlier ones when Jeannie was a student.

'This is our Bridget now,' said Nora.

'She really looks like you Jeannie,' Rico said.

'We used to knock about a lot when we were kids. What's she doing now?'

Tales were swopped, but none of the people seemed real to Kitty. What did it matter? In two weeks time they would be on their way back home. All they were were forgotten names, without bearing on each other's lives. She felt utterly desolate, lonely and unimportant.

Rico was excited. 'Why don't we phone up England?'

'What the hell will that cost?' Kitty asked, feeling annoyed with him. Why should he be part of anything over in England. She wanted him to stay separate and apart. He already had her daughter. She might have come home if it wasn't for him. She forced herself to smile when he asked her where her spirit of adventure was.

'To hell with the expense!' He said gallantly, giving her the receiver. 'You're our guests!'

Kitty felt as if she was lost.

'Here Jeannie,' she said, the heart gone out of her. 'You do it.'

In London it was nearly two in the morning when the phone began to ring. Bridget had been sleeping badly for the past few nights and so was not sure if she heard it or not. There seemed to be bells ringing all day sometimes. It drove her mad. But this time it kept on until she was awake and rushing to the living room in shock, leaving a trail of lights down the stairs. One day she really would get that extension put in, she told herself angrily as she took a coat off the hall-stand to drape around her.

'All right, all right,' she said. God, whoever it was they seemed to want to wake up the entire house. She flicked the table lamp on and blinked in its yellow light with eyes that felt gummy and stung from the brightness. Pushing the lamp from her she turned her face away.

'Hello?'

'Hi!' said a voice with just a trace of Liverpool while the phone crackled. 'This is Jeannie Moran, Kitty's daughter. I'm ringing from Los Angeles. I've got your mom here, here she is!'

Jeannie's voice sound tinny. She moved out of range leaving Bridget listening to the stillness of the sleeping house and the gurgling noises from the phone. She heard bumps and crashes magnified and heard her mother shouting 'For God's sake!'

She giggled, knowing her mother's distrust of telephones for she was uneasy with all machinery and Bridget could well imagine the struggle at the other end as she would try to let Kitty go first. She had not expected them to ring. She thought that she would get a postcard in her mother's shaky handwriting.

'Hello?'

Bridget jumped at the sound of her mother's voice. It was no different than when she phoned from London, but the sense of distance this time of a *real* distance not imagined, terrified and shocked her.

Her mother talked on and on, describing the flight and the food and the flat and Jeannie's hair. She was excited, bubbling like a school girl. Bridget suddenly felt upset. It crossed her mind that if her mother weren't to come back . . . but that was ridiculous! Still it made her uncomfortable. But if she didn't come back . . . she could not entirely brush away the wild idea.

'Here's our Kitty.'

'Hello love,' Kitty sounded sober, even a little dull.

'Hello Aunt Kitty. You sound tired.'

'It's all this travelling. I'm no spring chicken.'

Bridget laughed.

'What time is it there?' Kitty asked.

'Here? Two in the morning,' and there was a silence.

Kitty was stunned. The lost hours that she had read about had really happened only it had worked in reverse, she had grown older. They had lost part of the day and part of themselves that they could never reclaim.

Two in the morning. Kitty felt that between them were mountain ranges, lakes, the Atlantic ocean that their forebearers had sailed. She was in the new world that she had never expected to see. People did strange things like bringing dinner home in paper containers. There were babies born and the old ones dying. Lost time.

Bridget felt disorientated. She could imagine herself drifting out towards the landmass, out towards her aunt's voice. She had not had enough sleep for days and her head was beginning to throb.

In Downtown Los Angeles the rained-on pavement shone like a cold mortuary slab offering a resting place to the glass shattered rags that huddled in doorways. Still pan-handling, the old pioneers in the land of the free.

Two in the morning. Kitty wondered if the music ever stopped or the flash, flash, flash of the neon lights. The cars never stopped running. Endless miles of freeway dissected the land. Tomorrow they would drive down to the coast and listen to the breakers roaring across the ocean and pretend that they had not heard the lost time reaching out, channelled into a telephone mouthpiece. Vastness had opened up between them, sightless and yawning. She had lost Jeannie.

'Hey love,' Kitty said to Bridget, 'I just want to come home.' Her voice was mournful, almost a lament. Then she added quickly, as an afterthought: 'Don't say anything to your mother will you, she's having *such* a good time.'

SHEBA FEMINIST PUBLISHERS

Sheba is a racially mixed publishing co-operative formed in 1980. We prioritise writing by Black women, working class women, new writers and lesbians, and publish anti-sexist, anti-racist children's books.

Our most recent titles include:

A Burst of Light
Essays by Audre Lorde/£4.95

Lorde's first collection of essays since 1984 illuminates living life to the fullest in the presence of death. Courageous, wise, and once again battling cancer, Audre Lorde is essential reading.

Talking Back – Thinking Feminist/Thinking Black
bell hooks/£5.95

The Author of *Ain't I a Woman: Black Women and feminism* and *Feminist Theory: From Margin to Centre*, bell hooks confirms her position as one of the most exciting and inspiring Black feminist writers today.

Serious Pleasure – Lesbian Erotic Stories and Poetry
Edited by the Sheba Collective/£5.95

Over fifteen short stories make up this sensuous, arousing, exciting, daring, witty, and subtle collection.

Charting the Journey: An Anthology of Black and Third World Women's Writings, ed. Shabnam Grewal, Jackie Kay, Liliane Landor, Gail Lewis, Pratibha Parmar

Exciting new anthology bringing together the experiences of many different Black and Third World women who are, or have been based in Britain. In stories, poems, articles, interviews and sketches, these women bring forth issues pertinent to our lives. Long overdue, *Charting the Journey* covers the various journeys, both emotional and physical that we have all made. Visions of the future bind these pieces together and the voices speak out loud. Powerful and affirming.

Published March 1988
ISBN 0 907179 33 9
£7.95

Good Enough to Eat, Lesléa Newman

Liza is obsessed with food and weight. Her life is dominated by alternating binges and diets, each one creating, yet again, the need for the other. Lesléa Newman has written a novel which takes the issues of women, food, and weight seriously and yet manages to be extremely funny, especially when dealing with Liza's relationships with men and her growing fascination with the possibility of loving women. A pleasure to read!

Published April 1987
ISBN 0 907179 43 6
£4.95

Turning the Tables: Recipes and Reflections from Women, compiled by Sue O'Sullivan

American cornbread and black-eyed peas, Iraqi pepper salad, Ghanaian chicken, prawn pilau and more: a mouthwatering multitude of recipes. But that's not all! Accompanying the directions for these favorite dishes are riveting personal reflections on food, encompassing childhood, class influence, migration, ambivalence about cooking and eating, guilt, sensuality, sexuality, politics: everything is sacred. Includes contributions from Jewelle Gomez, Julie Christie, Linda Bellos and many other women. It is beautifully illustrated and has a comprehensive index. This cookbook with a difference is as much a kitchen book as a bedtime book!

Published November 1987
ISBN 0 907179 38 1
£5.50

Other Books by Audre Lorde

Our Dead Behind Us
In this challenging and extraordinary new collection, Audre Lorde gives us poems that explore, 'differences as creative tensions, and the melding of past strength/ pain with future hope/fear, the present being the vital catalyst, the motivating force — activism.' As Marilyn Hacker has written, 'Black, lesbian, mother, cancer survivor, urban woman: none of Lorde's selves has ever silenced the others; the counterpoint among them is often the material of her strongest poems.' That counterpoint here becomes a compelling force for change.
Published May 1987
ISBN 0 907179 27 4
£3.95

Zami: A New Spelling of My Name
Zami blends together history, biography and myth, telling a story that stretches from the Harlem of Audre Lorde's girlhood, in the 1930's, to the Greenwich Village of the 50's. It offers rare glimpses of a Black child's perception of World War Two; a Black woman's fear in the McCarthy era; of how it was to be a Black lesbian in the 50's. *Zami* joins the ranks of classic reading by Black women about Black women.
Published June 1984
ISBN 0 907179 26 6
£4.95

The Cancer Journals
Audre Lorde writes of her experience of mastectomy with honesty, precision and passion. This book is sure to give comfort and validation to women who have had breast cancer, to women who have feared it, to women who are scared of death itself. This is an innovatory book: breaking the silence that shrouds cancer, exposing the travesty of prothesis, Lorde pulls out the positive from her pain.
Published September 1985
ISBN 0 907179 34 7
£2.95

Other titles from Sheba include:

Aditi and the One-Eyed Monkey, a modern fairy-tale by Suniti Namjoshi/£2.95

A Burst of Light by Audre Lorde/£4.95

The Cancer Journals by Audre Lorde/£2.95

Changing Images, anti-racist, anti-sexist drawings by Natalie Ninvalle/£2.00

Charting the Journey, an anthology of Black and third world women's writing/£6.95

A Dangerous Knowing, four British Black women poets/£2.95

Feminist Fables by Suniti Namjoshi/£3.95

Gifts from My Grandmother, poetry by Meiling Jin/£2.95

Girls are Powerful, an anthology of young women's writing/£3.75

The Great Escape of Doreen Potts, a children's book by Jo Nesbitt/£2.50

Marge, a psychic thriller by Kitty Fitzgerald/£3.75

Our Dead Behind Us poetry by Audre Lorde/£3.95

Our Own Freedom, a photographic essay on women in Africa by Maggie Murray and Buchi Emecheta/£3.75

The Playbook for Kids about Sex, a workbook for children by Joani Blank and Marcia Quackenbush/£2.00

A Simple Mistake, a novel by Dorothy Grey/£4.95

The Things That Divide Us, short stories by North American women writers/£4.95

The Threshing Floor, short stories and a novella by Barbara Burford/£4.95

Through the Break: Women and Personal Struggle edited by Pearlie McNeill, Marie McShea, and Prathiba Parmar/£6.95

True to Life, writings by young women/£4.95

Turning the Tables: Recipes and Reflections from Women, compiled by Sue O'Sullivan/£5.50

We are Mesquakie, a young people's novel by Hadley Irwin/£2.75

Zami: A New Spelling of My Name, an autobiographical novel by Audre Lorde/£4.95

A free catalogue is available upon request.

SHEBA will be pleased to supply you books direct to your door! Simply fill in the form below, enclose your cheque and return to:

SHEBA FEMINIST PUBLISHERS
10A BRADBURY STREET
LONDON N16 8JN

QTY	TITLE	Price per book	TOTAL

Add 10% (p&p)
TOTAL DUE £

I enclose a cheque/postal order for £ ....
Please send my books to: ....

NAME: ....

ADDRESS: ....

....

....

Post Code

☐ Please add my name to SHEBA's mailing list.